John Francome has been Champion Jockey seven times and is regarded as the greatest National Hunt jockey ever known. James MacGregor is the pseudonym of a practising barrister, who also has an avid interest in racing.

Their successful writing partnership has produced four bestselling novels, including *Eavesdropper*, *Blood Stock* and *Declared Dead*, which have gained enthusiastic critical acclaim:

'The racing feel is authentic and it's a pacy, entertaining read' *The Times*

'. . . their best book so far' *Mail on Sunday*

'A thoroughbred stayer . . . cracking thriller' *Independent*

Riding High

John Francome
& James MacGregor

HEADLINE

First published in 1987
by Macdonald & Co (Publishers) Ltd

First published in paperback in 1988
by Futura Publications

Reprinted in this edition in 1993
by HEADLINE BOOK PUBLISHING

10 9 8

ISBN 0 7472 4127 9

Typeset by Keyboard Services, Luton

Printed and bound in Great Britain by
Mackays of Chatham plc, Chatham, Kent

HEADLINE BOOK PUBLISHING
A division of Hodder Headline PLC
338 Euston Road
London NW1 3BH

Riding High

Chapter 1

'*Allez, Maurice, allez!*' screamed a garlic-assisted voice into Alistair Rye's ear as the runners in the Grand Prix de Deauville rounded the final right-handed bend and galloped into the home straight. Philanderer, owned by Alistair's employer, Wayne Morrow, was still in the lead but its five-length advantage was rapidly disappearing as Maurice Boucher, the champion French jockey and darling of the Deauville crowd, urged the favourite, Fille de Joie, forward. Beside the French filly, and apparently going equally as well, was the English-owned Rough Diamond. It was now obvious that the finish was going to be a very close-run thing.

Entering the final furlong the three runners had drawn well clear of the rest of the field and even more importantly Jose Ramirez, Philanderer's jockey, had kept his position on the rails. With

Rough Diamond beginning to tire beside her, Fille de Joie was hedged in beside the rail with evidently plenty of running in her but nowhere to go. Alistair gripped his binoculars tightly in amazement as Ramirez suddenly and for no obvious reason switched his whip into his right hand and smacked Philanderer sharply on the side of the neck. The horse responded by swerving to his left, leaving a gap big enough for a Metro which Maurice Boucher accepted gratefully.

'You idiot,' Alistair shouted out loud, his anger drowned by the noise of the spectators around him.

But then, just as suddenly, Ramirez closed the gap and Philanderer and Fille de Joie were locked together, wither to wither, with Boucher's right leg jammed against the running rail. For what seemed a lifetime, but was in reality only a matter of seconds, he clung on to his filly's neck before sliding down to the ground and colliding with a post. As the French jockey lay motionless Philanderer galloped on and passed the finishing line to the boos and screams of the disbelieving crowd.

Morrow, who was standing beside Alistair, put down his binoculars and turned angrily to his racing manager.

'What the hell was that guy up to? Of all the dumb acts. The stewards are bound to take the race from us.'

'For absolutely certain. Yes, there it is.'

'*Enquête,*' boomed a voice over the loudspeaker to a roar of approval.

'That's if Ramirez survives the crowd. They're going mad down there.'

Alistair pointed from their position in the grandstand down to where an anxious-looking stable lad was trying to lead Philanderer from the racecourse along a dirt track which led over to the winners' enclosure behind the grandstand. Screaming hordes of outraged French racegoers were shaking their fists and no doubt shouting abuse at Jose Ramirez. From nowhere a group of armed policemen had appeared to add their contribution to an already threatening situation. Ramirez's attitude did not improve the atmosphere. Dressed in the famous Morrow colours of yellow with a red tassel on the cap, his face betrayed nothing but contempt for the angry punters around him and as Alistair watched through his binoculars he could have sworn that Ramirez spat at least twice in the mob's direction.

'Come on, Wayne. We'd better get down there and find out what happened. It looks like your favourite jockey has taken leave of his senses.'

Together they made their way behind the grandstand across the garden area which led to the unsaddling enclosure in front of the weighing room. The last Sunday of racing at Deauville's famous August meeting had attracted thousands of holiday-makers and it took some time for them to force their way into the enclosure. Inside, inspecting the horses, stood a group of earnest well-groomed Frenchmen shaking their heads knowingly, as if to say, what else could you expect from foreigners. Jose had already dismounted and was evidently on the receiving end of a torrent of abuse from Etienne Lafayette, Philanderer's trainer. The young Frenchman was as immaculately attired as ever – the perfect formation of the creases on his face suggested that he had even accompanied his suit to the cleaners. Raising his hands to the sky in despair he turned towards Morrow and Alistair.

'Monsieur Morrow, the man is an idiot. He refuses to offer any explanation for this . . . this imbecility. He just hisses at me through his teeth and a moment ago he spat at me. He must go. You must sack him. There is no way he can ride Philanderer in the Arc.'

The Frenchman's dislike of Ramirez was nothing new, but since Ramirez had been chosen by Morrow to be his retained jockey in Europe and since Morrow paid the not-too-insignificant training fees, even Etienne had reluctantly accepted the maxim that he who pays the piper calls the tune. Alistair for his part would have been delighted to see the back of the little Mexican. There was something about him which he too thoroughly disliked. The small wrinkled sallow face with its evil expression was accentuated by two narrow eyes which looked as if they had been added on as an afterthought.

Jose just scowled at them, said nothing and then spat on the ground. His insolence was not lost on the jeering, disgruntled men and women who were leaning over the railing separating the enclosure from the public area.

'Get him out of my sight,' said Morrow. 'Alistair, this inquiry is a foregone conclusion. I'm going to leave for Paris right now. The plane's waiting and this way I can make a couple of calls from my hotel room and turn in for an early night. Walk me to the car. I want to have a word with you about our little Mexican friend there.'

Morrow and Alistair made to leave, and as they did so the American was struck in the face by a copy of *Paris Turf*, the French racing paper. '*Cochon!*' screamed a fat and obviously highly volatile Frenchwoman, her black dress straining at its contents. Ceremoniously she ripped up a ticket for the pari-mutuel and threw the pieces over her shoulder. Morrow just smiled and murmured, '*Pardon, Madame*' before walking quickly towards the exit from the course.

As always, Morrow's instructions were precise and brooked no discussion.

'Alistair, I've decided not to renew Ramirez's retainer for next season. I want you to have him up to the villa after the races and give him the bad news. Tell him that he can still ride Philanderer in the Arc, that's if the French authorities let him keep his licence. Try to be nice about it. I don't want him going round bad-mouthing me to the press. Okay?'

Alistair nodded. He was in no position to argue. Only a year ago he had been bankrupt and without a job. The chance to be Morrow's racing manager had come out of the blue and he and his wife Claudia had grabbed the opportunity with both hands.

'When are you coming back to the States?' Morrow asked.

'Well, Claudia and I planned to fly back on Tuesday. I'm seeing Jack Donnelly tonight and I thought we could discuss our plans for the yearling sales. Claudia's keen to go to the casino tonight and then have one last day on the beach. You know women!'

In fact that was an understatement. Morrow had been married and divorced three times.

'I sure do. Look after that girl, Alistair. She's too pretty to let out loose on her own.'

'Don't worry, I will.'

Morrow grinned and climbed into the back of his waiting chauffeur-driven limousine.

'I'll phone you later from Paris to see how things go. Good luck this evening!'

'Thanks,' muttered Alistair to himself as he waved goodbye. A face-to-face confrontation with Ramirez was about as pleasant a prospect as a slow dance with a rattlesnake.

He decided to walk back to the weighing room to leave Ramirez a message to come and see him at La Cage at 6.15. It was now just past 3.30 and with a bit of luck the Mexican would still be in with the stewards. He felt distinctly nervous about the proposed meeting. The jockey had treated him with ever-increasing contempt since the racing season had begun and sometimes gave the impression that he had some kind of hold over him. Just precisely what, Alistair could never fathom as there was no way Ramirez could know about Alistair's betting coups, and even then they had been the product of inside information and not of any dishonesty on his part. What's more, none had

7

been on any Morrow-owned horses or even in races in which Morrow had had a runner. One thing was certain: he would be glad not to have to act any longer as the delivery boy for the additional cash payment which Ramirez had demanded on top of his generous retainer. In many ways he was surprised that Morrow had gone along with the Mexican's requests, but presumably if you make millions on the stock market you become used to the odd piece of unusual or greedy behaviour. After all, Ramirez had been one of the top jockeys in New York and with his famous crouching action had won numerous big-stake races. It was just unfortunate that his riding that season in Europe had become increasingly unreliable. Occasionally he had given the appearance of being in another world; he often seemed distracted and almost contemptuous of his riding instructions. His performances in the saddle had recently bordered on the lethargic, yet they could not be attributed to wasting. He was only five feet tall and had no difficulty in going to scale at eight stone, or just under 51 kilos as the French would say.

At least, Alistair consoled himself, the meeting was bound to be fairly short, and he could always look on the positive side of his job. An apartment in New York, daily contact with the world he loved and the chance to oversee a racing empire with over one hundred and fifty horses, including one hundred divided among trainers in France, Italy, Ireland and England. Who knows, one day Morrow might even give him the chance to train again. Claudia, he reflected, might not be so keen but he would just leap at the chance. He had succeeded before, and there was no reason why he could not succeed again. But this time he would make sure that he did not have owners like Max Stride, with all the morality of a polecat. What a sickening twist of fate that it should be Stride who owned Rough Diamond and who would now benefit from Ramirez's antics and Philanderer's inevitable disqualification.

He walked past the somewhat shabby parade ring on his right and soon reached the weighing room. Happily Ramirez was still in with the stewards. Although the jockeys for the next race had long gone, and the general preparations were well under way, there were still groups of owners and trainers talking excitedly about the finish to the big race. From his limited grasp of French, Alistair gathered that Boucher had, it was feared, sustained serious injuries to his back in the fall, and the ambulance whose siren he had just heard had taken him off to hospital. He was plainly in no condition to give evidence at the inquiry, but it was scarcely needed. It had looked bad enough from the grandstand, and the evidence of the head-on camera was bound to be damning.

Alistair was just looking for some paper to write a note on when suddenly Ramirez appeared, wearing an even more belligerent expression than usual.

'What happened, then?' asked Alistair.

'The bastards have stood me down for four weeks and fined me ten thousand francs.'

'And the horse?'

The Mexican laughed. 'The horse? Your owner's favourite pet has been disqualified.'

Alistair swore to himself. The result was inevitable but that didn't make its confirmation any the more palatable; 500,000 francs of prize money down the drain, and even greater potential damage done to the horse's value as a stallion. He tore into the jockey.

'What the hell do you think you were doing, coming off the rails like that in the first place? And then nearly killing Boucher?'

'I don't need riding lessons from you. If Morrow's got a complaint, he can give it to me in person later.'

'I'm sorry to disappoint you but he wants me to see you this evening at La Cage at 6.15.'

'What about? He's not trying to get rid of me, is he, the bastard?'

10

'Cut out the insults, Ramirez. I don't intend to discuss it with you here.'

Their raised voices were beginning to attract attention and Alistair stopped, remembering Morrow's warnings about adverse publicity.

Fortunately, or not so fortunately as it transpired, Etienne Lafayette arrived just at that moment. The French trainer instantly flew into a torrent of high-pitched insults directed at Ramirez, finishing with a dramatic thump of his right hand on a nearby table. The Mexican remained impassive throughout, waiting for the end of the onslaught before spitting on the floor and arrogantly wiping his mouth with the sleeve of his racing silks. Alistair just had time to intervene as Lafayette, losing all control of his temper, moved forward as if to strike him.

'Leave this to me, Etienne. Jose, come to La Cage at 6.15. Is that clear?'

The Mexican said nothing, turned away and strode into the changing room.

Chapter 2

La Cage was a large and beautiful villa set back from the coastal road which leads from Deauville to the fishing port of Honfleur. Standing on a hillside, it commanded a magnificent view of the sea, and when the sun shone Alistair found it hard to believe that England was only fifty miles away across the Channel. Wayne Morrow had taken the villa for the whole of August, the month when Deauville was the mecca of French racing. Almost every day there was flat-racing either at the famous Deauville course or on the smaller, and some would say far prettier, course on the outskirts of the town, called Clarefontaine. All the famous French trainers and a good number of English ones ran their horses, and the town was jammed with the disgustingly rich, the very wealthy and the less fortunate who were forced to live off the interest on their capital. Happily it was also crammed with enthusiastic punters and other holidaymakers, many of whom preferred to spend their time sunbathing on Deauville's wide and seemingly never-ending beach. And in the evening there were always the casinos – one in Deauville, the other a dice throw away in Trouville.

La Cage had been built in the early twenties and boasted marble floors and extravagant floral wallpaper. Alistair was not much of an expert on art but even he could recognise one or two of the signatures on the paintings which covered the walls. The contents of the house, including the fine mahogany furniture, were clearly worth a fortune, but surprisingly there were no visible signs of any security system. Perhaps the owners reasoned that the presence of armed guards at the front door would only excite the interest of burglars. It had come as no surprise when Morrow had told him that the rent was $15,000 and that was per week!

When he arrived at the villa, Claudia was still in her dressing-gown, lying on the chaise longue in the drawing room. She had taken to a life of luxury like tomato ketchup to a hot dog, and had not shown the slightest regret at giving up the role of

14

trainer's wife. When she had met Alistair she had been at drama school, and irrespective of whether she could act, her stunning looks and long auburn hair were enough to captivate any audience, at least of men. Now, thanks to Morrow's generosity, she had been able to return to acting school in New York, and Alistair had resigned himself to the not-too-distant prospect of lonely evenings whilst she trod the boards in some smoky theatre off-Broad-way. She was reading Jackie Collins' latest novel, a cigarette in the other hand. On the table beside her stood a glass of what looked like a Bellini – champagne and peach juice. The half-empty bottle of Krug on the floor suggested that this wasn't by any means her first drink that afternoon.

'Darling,' she cried, 'you're back early. Nothing wrong, is there?'

'Plenty! The horse won, but that weirdo Ramirez couldn't resist the temptation of trying to put another jockey over the rails en route. The long and short of it is that we were disqualified, Ramirez has been stood down for twenty-eight days, and the French jockey is in hospital nursing a broken back, or something just as ghastly. Oh yes, and Wayne has gone off early to Paris leaving yours truly to give the Mexican the heave-ho.'

'What, tonight?'

'Yes, tonight. Here at 6.15, or whenever *el gran señor* condescends to appear.'

'Why you? Why can't Wayne do his own dirty work?'

'Because, my love, that is the lot of racing managers, at least of this particular one. Doing the nasty bits while the boss collects the trophies.'

'At least you hate the little rat, so that'll make it easier for you.'

'That's true, but there's something irrational about him which worries me. I keep on thinking he knows something I don't. It's almost as if he's laughing at me.'

'Don't be ridiculous. He's never had an original thought in his life. What you think is cunning is just the tortuous process of his brain trying to conjure up a complete sentence.'

'What about that sneer he always has on his face?'

'Don't be so absurd. It's probably just a nervous reaction – you know, like your mother's headache whenever she has to do the washing up.'

Alistair chose not to rise to the bait. 'He won't be here for a couple of hours. I think I'll go and read in the garden for a bit.'

'Good idea. It might calm you down. You remind me of how you used to get before, when we had a fancied runner. Anyone would've thought that it was you who was going to have to sprint six furlongs. Can I stay to watch the execution or would you rather have me out of sight?'

'I'd prefer you to stay. I may need a witness in case it turns nasty. He was pretty rude to me in the weighing room just now.'

'You don't think he'll get vicious, do you? These Latins are so temperamental. How exciting!'

'I'm glad you like the idea. I expect he'll just swear, or give me one of those looks of his. Anyway, Wayne has asked me to do it nicely and avoid a scene. He's worried about bad publicity.'

'Is he sacked as from now?'

'No. For some reason Wayne still wants him to ride Philanderer in the Arc, and the way the horse ran today, only three-quarters fit, means he has a real chance. I've got to tell him that Morrow has decided not to use a retained jockey next season, and for that reason alone his services will no longer be required.'

'I get it. This-hurts-me-more-than-it-hurts-you routine. You men are all the same. Never tell the truth if a lie lets you sleep more easily.'

'Claudia, there are times when I think you are a prize bitch.'

She grinned. 'And what about the other times?'

17

'What I think then is a matter between me and the confessional.'

'But you're not even a Catholic! Go on, spoil me!'

'Later. In the meantime I'm going to relax. Do me a favour and wake me at six if I fall asleep.'

As he dozed off he could hear the phone ringing in the distance. He left it for Claudia to answer.

Forty minutes or so later she was upstairs changing when the door bell rang. As it was the maid's day off, Alistair went to let the Mexican in himself, still feeling more than a little apprehensive about the impending encounter. Ramirez was dressed in a cream suit and a pink open-necked shirt, with an enormous gold medallion around his neck. No doubt it bore some suitable engraving on the reverse side. He followed Alistair into the drawing room and brusquely declined his offer of a drink.

'Can we make this quick?' he snapped. 'I've got a meeting at a quarter to eight and I'm going to have to walk to my place from here.' Ramirez had rented a small villa a mile down the road towards Honfleur.

'What's wrong with your car?'

'I crashed it during the week and the taxi that brought me out here refused to wait. The driver turned out to be a racing fan and was annoyed about what happened this afternoon. God, how I

18

hate these French peasants. So what's all the fuss about?'

Alistair was just about to launch into his re-hearsed speech when Claudia arrived. Her low-cut silk dress revealed more than a hint of a mag-nificent bronzed cleavage, the sight of which caused Alistair to loose his concentration.

'Er, it's like this,' he began to stutter. 'Jose, you know my wife of course: Claudia?'

'Sure. Get on with the message,' snapped the Mexican.

'Of course. Mr Morrow has been giving some thought to his riding requirements for next year and has decided, reluctantly, that he no longer wishes to have a retained jockey for his horses in Europe. He will therefore no longer need your services on a permanent basis. Naturally you will still have the ride on Philanderer in the Arc, and no doubt if you stay in France will have many rides on our horses next season.'

Ramirez said nothing. He just stood there, star-ing impassively at Alistair who, as the silence con-tinued, felt obliged to make further conversation.

'Of course I'm sure you understand.'

Plainly Ramirez didn't, as at that moment he spat in Alistair's face and burst out laughing.

'How dare you!' screamed Claudia, jumping from the sofa and moving towards them.

'You shut up, you little bitch!' replied Ramirez, pushing her away.

That was too much for Alistair. Instinctively his right fist lashed out, striking Ramirez just above the chin and breaking his upper lip. There was a gush of blood as the Mexican reeled backwards. In the next instant he had recovered, and was on the attack, throwing himself at Alistair and wrestling him to the floor. His long fingernails tore into Alistair's face, whilst Alistair tried to force up his chin in an attempt to throw him off.

'Let go of him!' screamed Claudia, but that only appeared to encourage the jockey. Although only five feet, he was fit, strong, vicious and determined.

For a moment Alistair managed to shove him to one side and together they rolled across the floor. Blood from Ramirez's cut was streaming over Alistair's face, mixing with that from his own scratch marks, and from a nasty gash which had opened up above his left eye. In the ensuing struggle Ramirez reached down and pulled something out from under the turn-up of his trousers.

'Look out!' cried Claudia. 'He's got a knife!'

The Mexican held the blade in his right hand as he threw himself at Alistair once more.

'For Christ's sake, pull him off!' he screamed to Claudia as he clutched the Mexican's wrist, bu̇ she was sobbing hysterically and seemed unable to move.

For a moment it seemed that the Mexican was winning. The knife was edging ever nearer to Alistair's throat. Then with a final desperate effort, Alistair twisted Ramirez's wrist and slowly but reluctantly the knife wobbled and fell to the floor.

Recovering her senses now, Claudia rushed over and kicked it out of the Mexican's reach. The two men broke apart and slowly rose to their feet.

'Get out, you bastard,' cried Alistair, 'before I call the police! Here, take your knife with you.' He picked it up and handed it back, the blade facing him.

Ramirez took out a handkerchief and wiped away the blood which was still dripping from his lips. Then he spat on to the carpet.

'You've not heard the last of this, Rye. If you think you can ditch me now you're wrong. I'll get you, and that bitch of a wife of yours!'

Instinctively, Alistair moved forward to hit him again, but this time Claudia intervened.

'Leave him. He's not worth it. Just a worthless punk.'

With the Mexican gone, Alistair poured himself and Claudia a large brandy.

'Jesus, that guy's a nut case. He could have

killed me. Did you see the look in his eyes? Do you believe all that stuff about revenge?'

'No, it's just a pathetic attempt to frighten you. Darling, you're bleeding horribly. Go upstairs and have a bath and I'll come and dress your wounds. Do you still want to go out to dinner with the Donnellys tonight?'

'I'll be fine in a while, but I don't think we'd better mention what happened just now, do you?'

Claudia hesitated. 'No, I think you're right. What are you going to tell Wayne?'

'What do you think?'

'I suppose he ought to know, but on the other hand, he might think you mishandled the situation, which wouldn't do you much good. On reflection I'd just say that Ramirez took it as badly as you anticipated.'

'Yes, I think you're right, though it makes me angry to think he's going to get away with it. On occasions like this I don't know where I'd be without your support.'

'On occasions like this you need a nurse, not a wife. Go on, have your bath and I'll come up and look after you. That cut above your eye is nasty. At least we can put the scratch marks down to a domestic dispute!'

'Can't we call it passion?'

'What will your friends think?'

22

Alistair laughed; having faced death a few minutes before, he was now experiencing an enormous feeling of relief.

'You still on for the casino afterwards?' he asked.

'You bet!' she replied. 'I've got this feeling that my luck's going to be in tonight.'

'I hope so. I'll give you a shout when I'm ready for my first aid. And in the meantime I'm going to have another drink. That man's spitting is enough to turn anyone to the bottle.'

Alistair was lying in the bath reflecting on his own heroics when he heard the phone ring. Five minutes later Claudia appeared to tell him that it was Morrow on the line from Paris, wanting to know how he got on with Ramirez.

'What did you tell him?'

'Very little. I thought it would be better coming from you.'

'Good. I'll get out and take it on the phone in the bedroom.'

'Well?' rasped Morrow. 'What happened?'

'What I expected. He wasn't best pleased and showed it. Didn't seem particularly enamoured at keeping the ride on Philanderer, but I expect he'll be more enthusiastic in the morning when he works out how much money is at stake.'

'Good. What are you up to tonight?'

'I'm having dinner with the Donnellys, and then

23

we thought we might have a final tilt at the roulette table. And you?'

'I'm settled in here at the Plaza. The television is incomprehensible so I guess I'll have an early night. See you in New York. Oh yes, I forgot to ask. I suppose we were disqualified?'

''Fraid so. And Ramirez was stood down for twenty-eight days.'

'Fool. We won't miss him next season.'

'We're agreed on that.'

'Right then. See you on Wednesday and good luck tonight.'

Half an hour later they were on their way to Beaumont en Auge and dinner.

Chapter 3

The Donnellys were already waiting for them
when they arrived at the restaurant and immediately commented on Alistair's appearance.
He muttered something about having walked into
a door at the villa, but while that might have
explained the cut above his eye, it still left the
scratch marks down the side of both his cheeks
unaccounted for.

'More likely you were hit by an angry French
punter after that performance this afternoon!
They would have lynched your man at Leopards-
town, and no jury would have convicted them,'
joked Jack Donnelly. 'I hope the big man's going to
give him the push now. He's been riding like a
clown all season.'

'Let's just say that the matter's under review.
Wayne's coming round to the idea of leaving it to

his individual trainers to decide who they put up. It will probably be far less hassle in the long run.'

'Sounds sensible to me. If you want my view, and you're going to get it anyway, that Ramirez is the type that's so crooked he can't lie straight in bed. There've been some nasty rumours floating round about him and the company he keeps. Take my word for it, you'll be well rid of him. I wouldn't even be surprised to hear he was tied up with this Eddie James business.'

'What Eddie James business?' asked Alistair eagerly. Eddie James was a well-known flat jockey whose riding career had recently taken a turn for the worse, culminating in the loss of his job with one of the more successful trainers.

'Haven't you heard? It was all over yesterday's *Sporting Life*.'

'Jack, you forget we're in France and there's not much demand here for the English runners and riders.'

'In which case I will fill you in with the gory details and in the meantime you girls can look at the menu and plan our assault on the talents of the chef here. The story is this. It appears that on his way back from York races a couple of weeks ago – you know, on the day when they ran The Matchmaker race – James was stopped by the

police on suspicion of driving under the influence.
Well, instead of going quietly and calling for a
lawyer, the silly sod kicked up a fuss, and in the
ensuing row tried to hit one of the boys in blue.
They then turned nasty, dragged him back to the
local nick, and strip-searched him. Lo and behold,
they find that he's got a package of heroin stuffed
down his trousers, and Eddie-boy's problems are
now just beginning.'

'Do you know where he got it from? Is he on the
stuff, or something?'

'How should I know? All I can tell you is what's
in the paper. He's been remanded in custody
pending police investigations, which suggests to
me that there could be more to come. There's a
rumour they want to interview all the jockeys who
were riding that day.'

'That would include Ramirez. We flew over
together in the morning for the big race, although
the way our horse ran we might just as well have
stayed at home. The police aren't likely to find him
very cooperative. A couple of grunts and the odd
spit are his idea of conversation. What other news
is there?'

The talk turned to the forthcoming sales of
yearlings in Ireland and England, at which Donnelly would be acting as an agent and adviser to

Morrow. The Irishman, for all his garrulousness and joviality, had a knack of spotting likely future winners and was considered by the racing fraternity to be a shrewd, hard-working and trustworthy man. His eye for a fast filly extended to women and the third Mrs Donnelly, some twenty years his junior and of very recent acquisition, was a vivacious girl from County Galway. When she laughed, and in Jack's presence that was inevitable, she threw her head back and her peals filled the room. Throughout the meal Jack regaled them with a string of hilarious and mainly obscene stories, and Alistair thought to himself that it was lucky that everyone else in the restaurant was French and probably couldn't understand.

They were on their third cognac and reminiscing when Teresa, Jack's wife, suddenly asked Alistair why he had given up training. 'I've asked Jack but he's told me it's none of my business.'

'And it still isn't,' said Jack, butting in.

'No, that's okay,' said Alistair. 'You're bound to hear it from somebody sooner or later, and since the truth is only known to a handful of people, and Jack is one of them, you might as well have the unexpurgated story from me. All I ask is that you don't tell anybody else. That is, as long as you two don't mind hearing it all again?'

'Not at all,' said Jack.

'Go on,' said Claudia. 'I'm going to the ladies' room anyway. I won't be long.'

'Well, as Jack may have told you, I used to have stables in Newmarket. I started six years ago in a small way and in my first season I had a bit of luck with a sprinter by Mummy's Pet. He'd been a very backward two-year-old and the owners moved him to me from Lambourn in the hope that the change of air might do the trick. That was one you missed at the sales, Jack. Probably below your price range. Anyway, by my third year I had over fifty horses and things were going very well. I had a regular jockey, Willie Grange, and some pretty big owners. One in particular, Max Stride, was very enthusiastic and money seemed to be no object. I trained some good winners and he rewarded me by buying horses each year at the sales. He paid his bills regularly, sometimes in cash, and seemed completely trustworthy. I had no idea where his money came from and never asked. He seemed to have money to burn. That year was also the year I married Claudia.

'One of Stride's horses won the Coventry Stakes at Royal Ascot, and he turned down a huge offer for it from the Arabs. He then started talking about stud farms and buying expensive yearlings, which as you can realise is music to any trainer's ears. Up to then the most I had ever paid was twenty thousand guineas – pocket money to you, Jack. Just over two years ago, Stride asked me to go to Keeneland for the sales – where incidentally, Teresa, your husband is famous for his after-dinner singing – and buy him a well-bred colt for up to $1,000,000. You can imagine how excited and nervous I was. I looked at every animal there and felt like a million dollars myself, having that kind of money to spend. I picked out four horses I liked and on the second day spent a million on a beautiful-looking colt by Nijinsky, out of an un-raced mare. I paid the bill myself with a banker's draft drawn on my own bank. My bank manager was very understanding and let me do that in the belief that I would be repaid by Stride as soon as I got back to England. I telephoned Stride straight away after the sale, from America, and he sounded a little awkward on the phone, but I knew he'd be delighted when he saw the animal. Anyway, to cut a long story short, the horse went berserk on the plane coming back over, after the flight had been delayed for three hours. It had to be destroyed, and lo and behold, I discover that Mr Stride had failed to insure the animal. Worse was to come when he denied ever giving me authority to buy it in the first place.'

'But surely you had something in writing?'

'It's easy to say that now, but he had always paid in the past, and I regarded his word as his bond. I therefore had to raise the money to pay off the debt, and that meant selling everything, including my stables. I only paid off the final instalment three months ago.'

'That's terrible. But surely you could have sued him? It was, after all, your word against his.'

Claudia now returned. 'Where've we got to?'

'Why I didn't sue Stride. Apart from the legal costs, which I couldn't afford, and the possible risk of losing, there was one other little problem.' Alistair paused and looked over towards Claudia.

'What was that?' asked Teresa.

'He told me that if I did, he would ensure that Claudia and I finished the rest of our lives in wheel-chairs.'

'Jesus Christ! Why didn't you tell the police?'

'Because they only take that kind of thing seriously when the threat has been executed. Claudia and I discussed it, and decided we would rather be poor and walking than rich and crippled. And then the offer came out of the blue from Wayne to be his racing manager, and now you know the rest. At least Claudia is spared the boredom of being a trainer's wife, and can now fulfil her dream to be the second Meryl Streep.'

31

'That's unfair, Alistair. Order another coffee and then we can go to the casino.'

'Can I just ask one more question?' said Teresa with half an eye anxiously on her husband.

'You be careful now, missus, with all your questions,' he cautioned, grinning at her.

'Go on,' said Alistair.

'What happened to Mr Stride? I suppose he's gone out of racing?'

'Where were you this afternoon? On the contrary, he has more horses in training than ever before. He'll almost certainly be at the casino tonight, whooping it up after Rough Diamond's victory today as a result of Philanderer's disqualification.'

Teresa sighed. 'There's no justice in this world.'

'We'll all drink to that,' said Jack, raising his glass.

Diamonds are certainly a croupier's best friend. The casino at Deauville is always packed in the summer season and never more so than when the racing set are in town. The huge main room was crammed with roulette and blackjack tables and in the middle of them all was a table reserved for chemin de fer, with a minimum banc of ten thousand francs; only multi-millionaires had the nerve and the funds to take part at those kind of stakes. When Alistair and the others arrived at just past midnight the casino was in full swing, each table crammed with anxious punters and a seemingly inexhaustible supply of ageing women, dripping with sapphires and emeralds. They particularly favoured the roulette wheel, eagerly writing down the winning number, in the conviction that there was more than just chance to the spin of the wheel, and that either fate, or the bias in the table, or the croupier's arm would reveal a discernible pattern. At the end of each table an ever-watchful overseer sat on a high chair – his job to watch both the croupiers and the punters, and to arbitrate on the not infrequent disputes as to whose chip was a winner. Alistair breathed in the magnificent atmosphere of greed and venality that pervaded the air. Any moment you expected a row to erupt, or temper to flare, as some player lost all on a final throw. Not all the habitués were rich. The most frenetic had an air of desperation and defeat as they wagered 500-franc chips on a single number, hoping against the odds for the 35 to 1 shot to come off.

Alistair had bought £100 worth of chips which he handed over to Claudia, and whilst she and the Donnellys sat down to play, he wandered round the room saying hello to familiar faces and enjoying watching the intent, almost demonic, expressions of the punters, as much as playing. Occasionally he noticed the odd glance in his direction, no doubt at the injuries to his face, but he no longer cared about the events earlier in the evening.

Madame de Vermeille, one of France's leading owners, waved at him from her seat beside one of the roulette tables and beckoned him over to join her.

'Alistair, darling!' she cried. She spoke in a very husky voice, the product, no doubt, of smoking too many of the cigarettes manufactured by her late and inordinately rich husband. 'Bring me some luck. This wretched croupier is determined I shall not win tonight.'

'Try number 22, it's my lucky number.'

She threw two 500-franc chips on to the table and shouted out her choice to the croupier. As he put the chips on for her, he shouted, '*Rien ne va plus*', and started the wheel spinning. The cry prompted a sudden flurry of betting, just as the announcement 'They're off' does in a betting shop. As if mesmerised, two dozen eyes followed the spin of the wheel as the little red ball bounced in and out of the numbered sockets, flirting first with one number then with another. Gradually the wheel began to slow and the movement of the ball became less frenetic. Then almost painfully the ball bobbled for the last time and came reluctantly to rest.

'*Vingt-deux*, twenty-two!' cried the croupier, to Madame de Vermeille's delight. The money, of course, meant nothing to her; the thrill of winning meant everything.

'Bravo!' she cried as the croupier clawed in all the losing chips with his shovel, leaving just the winners on the table to be paid out. A huge pile of chips was pushed towards Madame.

'*Pour la maison*,' she shouted, flicking a 500-franc chip in the direction of the croupier, who stuffed it down a special slit in the table.

Marvellous, thought Alistair to himself. A tip every time they win, but no reciprocal arrangement, of course, when they lose. He found it ironic that Madame's little act of generosity equalled half his own stake for the whole evening. Looking round the room he decided to go and watch the play on the chemin de fer table, which had just begun. There, seated at the middle of the table, looking as smug as a bookmaker who has had a skinner, was a familiar face. Max Stride was puffing away at a large Davidoff and plainly enjoying himself. Just at that moment, he looked up and caught Alistair's eye and a savage smirk crossed his face. There was no doubt about the man's outrageous good looks, and they had given him the confidence and arrogance of a matinée idol. He was in his late forties, but could have passed for younger. Well over six feet, he had a mass of black hair and a cherubic glow to his cheeks which was thoroughly misleading. Only the slight curl at the side of his wide mouth gave a hint of the evil personality of which Alistair had been the victim. One day, Alistair thought to himself, I'll fix you. But for the moment he was content to let that yearning for revenge brood in the warehouse of his mind.

He was just moving away to go and see how Claudia was getting on, when he felt a sharp prod in the crook of his back. He looked over his shoulder to see a large, seriously ugly man standing behind him.

'Mr Rye, would you please follow me?' he said, in a low voice which plainly wasn't at ease with the English language.

'Why?' asked Alistair, trying not to attract too much attention.

'Mr Hassan would like to have a few words with you in the bar.'

Alistair breathed in sharply. Hassan was the owner of Fille de Joie. A Moroccan with a string of horses and an extremely unsavoury reputation both on and off the course, he was unlikely to have been amused by that day's events and this summons probably meant that the proposed sale of one of his brood mares to Wayne Morrow was now off.

'I'm not sure I feel like talking to Mr Hassan at this moment,' he said, feigning disdain.

The messenger laughed. 'Then I will fire this gun I'm holding.'

'In that case, you have persuaded me and I'm delighted to come with you. Take me to your leader.'

Hassan was seated at a table in the corner of the bar – a large room with waiter service, on the other side of the hall to the gaming rooms. The table beside him was occupied by other members of his entourage, who by their size and appearance clearly did their thinking through their biceps.

'Mr Rye. Come and sit down. A drink, waiter, for my friend.' Alistair ordered a large whisky, deciding that he had at least to put on a brave face.

The Moroccan wasted no time with pleasantries. 'Mr Rye. I hate defeat. Winning the Grand Prix was something I have looked forward to all summer. Instead, my filly has been impeded disgracefully; I have lost a large prize; and my jockey is spending the next few days in hospital. Those things I can bear. The hurt to my honour, my pride, I cannot. At least, not easily. I have decided that I am still prepared to sell the brood mare to your

37

boss, but only if he pays me an additional $500,000 by way of compensation. Then I am prepared to forget this wholy ugly business.'

'What?' Alistair nearly choked on his whisky. 'Half a million dollars? It's not as if we won the race ourselves. If it's any consolation, we've already taken steps to deal with our jockey.'

'Just tell Mr Morrow that I want $500,000 compensation.'

'I'm sorry, but this may well mean that the deal is off.'

Hassan laughed. 'I don't think you understand me, Mr Rye. I want that money whether you buy the mare or not. You have cheated me, and nobody does that. Nobody, you understand.' He banged the table in anger.

'And if Mr Morrow doesn't agree?'

'We have a saying in Morocco that the hands of a thief are best separated from his body.'

Instinctively Alistair clenched his hands under the table, then rose to his feet.

'I'll pass on your message as soon as I return to America, but I warn you, he's not the kind of man to respond to threats.'

'Isn't he? Then we might have to start by making an example of *you*. I'll wait to hear from you. Good luck on the tables tonight.'

Alistair walked slowly back to the gaming room,

wondering what he had done to deserve such an evening. First Ramirez, and now Hassan. It only needed Stride to come up and threaten him, and he would, in racing jargon, have the treble up. He looked round for Claudia. She was no longer sitting next to the Donnellys, who, judging by the mountain of chips in front of the bloodstock agent, were on a winning run. He made up his mind to say nothing to Claudia about the latest threat. She was entitled to enjoy herself after what they had gone through together.

Surveying the room he spotted her. What the hell was she doing talking to Stride? Angrily he marched over towards them but before he could say anything Claudia spoke.

'Alistair. Mr Stride – Max – was offering us his commiserations over the race today.'

'Yes, Alistair, it was very tough on you, and it gave me no pleasure to win like that.' He smiled ingratiatingly.

You insincere little bastard! thought Alistair, but he said nothing.

'Look,' Stride went on, 'I know you still feel sore about that Keeneland business, but can't we now just shake hands and forget about it? How about if I made you an ex gratia payment of, say, £50,000, without admitting any kind of liability of course?'

Alistair looked at him in disbelief. If this was a

joke, it was in the poorest taste. If it was serious, it was the final insult from a man who had not the slightest understanding of guilt or the least notion of morality.

He grabbed Claudia by the arm. 'Come on, darling, we're going. There's a very nasty smell around here and it's not Madame de Vermeille's perfume.'

'Why were you so rude to him?' asked Claudia as they went down the long ornate staircase that led to the main doors.

'Rude? Under the circumstances, I thought I was polite. I very nearly hit him.'

'Darling, be honest. He's a foot taller than Ramirez and would probably have knocked you for six.'

'Don't you understand? That man nearly ruined our lives. He destroyed everything I worked for years to build up. To take charity from him now would be like, well, like taking blood from a man who had stabbed you.'

'But don't you see, that's the whole point. There are times when for survival you have to swallow your pride and take what's offered, whatever the source. Who knows, gradually he might pay it all off as his conscience gets to work on him. You're the one who wants to have children. How will we ever save enough to educate them properly? We can't make them live in the past as well, you know!'

They made the short drive home in silence.

Chapter 4

Alistair and Claudia flew back to New York on the
Tuesday, and the next day Alistair returned to
work at the headquarters of the Morrow Corpora-
tion. The offices were on the forty-second floor of a
large skyscraper half way up Fifth Avenue and
were surprisingly small, considering the size of
Morrow's financial empire. Morrow's philosophy
was to employ as few people as possible, and
instead to make his assets and money do the work
for him. His share dealings on Wall Street were
legendary, and he had the uncanny knack of being
able to spot take-over situations ahead of the field,
buying himself large blocks of shares to be sold out
later at a fat profit to the highest bidder. His motto
was 'Be a predator, not a creditor', and there was
no doubting his success. There were some who
considered that he gave capitalism a bad name,

but equally there was no doubting his philan-
thropic work. Not a day passed without some
charity receiving a sizeable contribution. That
wasn't to say that he was an easy man to deal with,
as Alistair had often noticed in the conduct of his
business affairs. Whilst he valued professional
advice, he liked to take all major decisions himself.
Alistair, like others, could propose, but it was for
Morrow to dispose, and anyone who thought otherwise did so at their peril.

Morrow was busy when Alistair arrived at work
that morning, and his secretary said she would call
him when he was free. Plainly some big deal was
cooking. Alistair was grateful for more time, as he
hadn't yet decided whether he should still keep
quiet about Ramirez's behaviour on Sunday or
whether he should pass on Hassan's demands. No-
one likes the bearer of bad news and Morrow was
no exception. In addition, Alistair was beginning
to worry about whether Ramirez could be relied
upon to ride Philanderer in the Arc – the last thing
he wanted was a bolshie jockey on the back of a
horse with a potential stud value running into
millions. Alistair decided that there could be no
harm in having a stand-by available, and the
obvious candidate was his old stable jockey, Willie
Grange. Willie, who had joined him as a raw

44

seventeen-year-old apprentice, had now developed into a fine jockey, with a cool head and an excellent sense of pace. He was very powerful in a finish, although happily his determination to win did not quite extend to putting other jockeys over the rails. Willie had been a true ally in Alistair's time of misfortune, and in his present job, as jockey to one of the biggest stables in the country, had supplied Alistair with some extremely useful information. That information had been translated into substantial winnings, which in turn had gone to pay off his bank debt.

Alistair looked at his watch. It was 3.30 in the morning over in England and Willie ought to be in bed asleep. If the jockey had one weakness, it was women, and while he might well be in bed, there was every chance that sleep was not the first thing on his mind. He was luckily still at an age when he could burn the candle at both ends without being singed.

Alistair dialled the number of Willie's flat in Newmarket. As he listened to the ringing tone, he began to regret his early-morning call, but before he could put the receiver down a voice had answered.

'Yes? Who the hell's that?'

'Willie, it's me, Alistair.'

45

'Bloody hell, do you know what time it is?'

'Sure. 9.30 and the weather here in Manhattan is sunny with hardly a cloud in the sky. I just wanted to say have a nice day.'

'You're joking, you must be. It's the middle of the night here, you oaf.'

'Darling, who is it?' Alistair could hear a girl's voice purring in the background. 'Only an old friend, kiddo. Go back to sleep,' whispered Willie.

'Okay, Alistair, what's the news in the Big Apple? I read about Philanderer losing that race on Sunday. That jockey of yours is a complete prat, and a dishonest one too if the rumours are correct.'

'What are they saying?'

'I'd rather tell you when I see you, but they say he's been pulling one or two recently. Is he going to keep the ride on Philanderer?'

'That's why I'm phoning. There's a possibility that he won't be on for the Arc, only a possibility I might add, and I was wondering whether you would be prepared to stand by?'

'Would I like hell. I'd love to. Hold on a moment. Look darling, not now, later. All right, I promise. Back to you, Alistair. These women have no sense of timing. Go on.'

'That's all I wanted to know. I'm seeing Morrow shortly, and I just want to put forward some contingency plans. If he gives the okay, I'll want you to come over to France some time before the race and ride the horse out. How's your luck at the moment?'

'Going well. I rode a treble at Ripon yesterday and at the moment I'm the guv'nor's blue-eyed boy.'

'Good, keep it up. What's all this I hear about Eddie James being caught with heroin?'

'Incredible, isn't it? There's all kinds of gossip round the track. There's some talk of him being part of a smuggling ring, but I don't believe it. The police are going to interview all the jockeys, which will be a laugh. Most of them think that heroin is somebody who's rescued by Clark Gable in an old black and white movie. Hey, stop that! Sorry Alistair, I've got to go and ride another winner. Keep in touch.'

Alistair killed the next hour reading reports from Morrow's trainers in England and Ireland on the respective horses in their charge, and planning the buying strategy for the forthcoming sales. This was the time of year when it was necessary to decide which horses were to be kept in training, which should be sold, and in particular which fillies should be used for breeding. All this in turn affected the number of yearlings to be bought, and once that was done, decisions had to be made as to who was to train them. In addition, Morrow had decided to expand his breeding interests and wanted to buy another stud, either in Ireland or England. Alistair had received a number of particulars in the post that morning. Prices were in the millions, and there were times when he could not but envy Morrow's spending power. Money breeds money, they say, and in Morrow's case it seemed that he was using a fertility drug.

At eleven o'clock he was called into the great man's presence. Morrow was seated behind his desk with his back to the window and a dramatic view of New York's skyline behind him. He was on the phone and shouting. 'Have you tried his flat? Yeah, and there's no reply?' He put his hand over the receiver and beckoned Alistair to sit down on the chair opposite him. 'It's Etienne from France. He says Ramirez hasn't turned up for the last three days to ride out.'

He returned to the call. 'Have you tried to reach him at Honfleur?'

Alistair could hear Etienne jabbering on in a mixture of French and English. 'You spoke to the cleaning lady who said she hadn't seen him since Saturday, but some of his clothes are still there? His bed hasn't been slept in? Okay, don't get hysterical. He's probably taken a holiday during his suspension and not bothered to tell us. Yes, I

48

know the man's an imbecile. Just console yourself with the thought that you won't have to worry about him next season. But for the moment he still rides Philanderer in the Arc. No, I see absolutely no reason to call the police in at this stage. Nor does Alistair who's here with me now, and nodding his head. Is that it? Good. *Au revoir.*'

Morrow put the phone down and shook his head in exasperation. 'Talk about fillies being highly strung. Will you deal with that maniac in future? I don't know what's more difficult – a poisonous Mexican, or a temperamental Frenchman.'

'How about a worried Englishman?'

Morrow laughed. 'There's nothing to be worried about. Ramirez will show up for certain. He's probably with some tart at the moment, living it up. Christ, what a ghastly thought. So what's your news?'

'Not much. I'm just a little concerned about relying on Ramirez in the Arc. It struck me that we should at least take the precaution of having a stand-by jockey and the sooner we make the necessary arrangements the greater the choice.'

'Do you have somebody in mind?'

'Yes, I do. I thought that Willie Grange would fit the bill. I've checked that he's available and he's ridden for you before.'

'Fine by me, but I've no doubt Ramirez will be

49

there on the day. No jockey is going to give up the chance of winning Europe's richest prize, and a share in Philanderer as a stallion.'

'I'd forgotten you'd promised him that as well.'

'He demanded it as a term of taking the job. These top jockeys really know how to screw you.'

Alistair shook his head. No wonder Ramirez had taken the loss of his retainer so badly.

Morrow seemed to be in a good mood, so Alistair decided to bite the bullet and pass on Hassan's message, albeit in a modified form.

'I'm afraid there's one other matter. Mr Hassan is not best pleased with what happened to Fille de Joie. He cornered me at the casino on Sunday night.'

'Don't tell me the price of the mare has doubled.'

'Worse, he wants a payment of $500,000 as compensation for the hurt to his pride.'

Morrow rose from his chair and turned to look out of the window.

'Does he now? If he thinks I'll pay that he can believe anything. What a jerk!'

Alistair had expected this reaction, but could not help feeling a surge of nausea at the thought of Hassan's minders carrying out their master's threats.

'I'm afraid he became rather threatening.'

'He did, did he? Well, I don't scare easily, and nor

do I expect my staff to. You can tell him that not only do I reject his suggestion; he can stuff his brood mare up the backside of a camel or whatever means of transport they have in Morocco.'

Alistair feigned a sickly smile. A racing manager's lot was obviously not always a happy one. Plainly now was not the time to go into details of the threats which had accompanied Hassan's proposal.

Alistair spent the afternoon arranging appointments to visit a number of potentially suitable studs when he went to England and Ireland for the bloodstock sales, and ringing Morrow's trainers in England to ask detailed questions about the horses in their care. As far as Morrow was concerned, horse racing was first and foremost a business and he never tired of saying that it cost the same amount to train a bad horse as a good one. Of course all trainers knew this, but considering the shortage of good horses and the fact that training was their livelihood you could not really blame them for being optimists. It was a rare and brave trainer who had the courage to tell an owner to take a horse away because its earnings would never match its training fees. After all, there can only be six winners at most race meetings!

He decided to walk home across Central Park, a

hazardous exercise at night but relatively safe during the day. As always there were a fair number of joggers, their faces straining in the excitement of getting fit, but his thoughts so preoccupied him that he hardly noticed his surroundings. He pictured Willie Grange in bed with some glamorous well-built blonde and no doubt with a different girl tomorrow and every other night of the week. Before he married Claudia, he too had chased girls, but not with anything like Willie's success rate. Five feet eight and squarely built, he did not have the kind of striking looks or physique which made a woman throw caution to the wind, even for one night. He remembered how at teenage parties all the girls were always attracted to the strong silent type sitting wistfully in the corner, puffing away at a cigarette and staring melancholically into the distance like a budding Clint Eastwood. That was always taken to denote strength of character or depth of feelings, whereas he believed that the real reason was the lonely figure had absolutely nothing to say.

He was happy with Claudia, or at least he told himself he was. They had met at a New Year's Eve party when she was still at drama school in London, and determined to be an actress. She was extremely sexy with a wicked smile and what one of his friends had described as bedroom eyes. He had been surprised when she had let him take her out, and astonished when she had accepted his proposal of marriage. To her credit she had knuckled down to the job of trainer's wife and when it came to chatting up the owners there was none better. He was never certain whether her apparent enthusiasm was genuine or just another polished performance, but whether the owner was a publican's wife with a quarter share in a selling plater, or Max Stride with his string of thorough-breds, her bonhomie was always the same. She had been a brick during the Keeneland fiasco and he did not begrudge her obvious enjoyment of their new life. Recently she had auditioned for a number of roles and soon, no doubt, would get lucky. His only sadness was that it inevitably meant the further postponement of a family.

By now he had crossed the park and reached the apartment block where they lived. Feeling ener-getic he declined the lift and rushed up the stairs, wondering what Claudia would think of Ramirez's disappearance. He opened the door and fittingly he was hit by the smell of Mexican cooking. Walking into the drawing room-cum-dining room he found that the table had already been laid with a dozen roses neatly arranged on top of a linen tablecloth.

'Hey, who are you expecting for dinner?' he shouted in the direction of the kitchen. 'Do you

have some secret lover and is this the way of
breaking the news to me?'

As he walked towards the kitchen she appeared
in a black cocktail dress with an apron over it. She
smiled.

'Damn it, you're early. I just thought we'd have a
little celebration.'

For a fleeting moment Alistair thought she
might be pregnant. 'You're not . . .' he began, but
she seemed not to hear him as she continued, 'It's
just wonderful. I've landed a part in a new play.
Just think of it, my first paid role!'

He hid his disappointment. 'Darling, that's marvellous news. But you didn't tell me you were
auditioning today.'

'I'm sorry, but I decided that telling you might
have been bringing me bad luck. I know that sort
of thing is rubbish but you know how superstitious
I am.' She grabbed his arm and led him towards the
sofa.

'Well then, aren't you going to tell me all about
it?' he asked.

'Of course I am, but I wanted to make this
moment last. It's in a new play about a husband
who runs off with his wife's best friend and the wife
then discovers she's dying. It's by a young, very
sensitive writer and if it all goes well it'll transfer
to Broadway.' She clapped her hands with glee.

'The plot sounds a little gloomy,' said Alistair.

'Oh, I knew you'd say that. Unless you can sing along or laugh, you hate the theatre. You remind me of that American woman who said she didn't like *Hamlet* because of all the quotes.'

'That's not true. I like Shakespeare as much as the next man, but after you've been up at five-thirty every morning and driven fifteen hundred miles in a week, you tend to lose interest in the accuracy of witches' predictions, except that they tend to be more reliable than racing tipsters'.'

'Why are you always so flippant? There are times when I despair.'

'Darling, I'm sorry. I really am pleased for you, honestly. When do you start rehearsals?'

'Next week, and we open in the middle of October.'

Alistair's face fell. 'Does this mean you can't come over for the Arc and then for the sales?'

'I'm sorry, darling, but I know you'll manage all right without me. It'll give you a chance to chat up all those girls you fancy.'

'And who's backing this venture?'

'I don't know, but he's meant to be very rich and money's no object.'

'Sounds like he ought to go into racing. This calls for champagne, I'll go out and get a bottle.'

'No need. I've already bought one. It's in the fridge. Oh Alistair, I'm so, so happy.'

'And I'm happy for you, darling.'

They dined together by candle-light and Alistair could not help being pleased to see his wife looking so elated. He realised that this inevitably meant seeing even less of her, with lonely evenings spent waiting for her to return after the night's performance. Even worse was the idea of their home being over-run by a lot of arty types, smoking pot, nodding their heads earnestly, discussing the merits of this director or that one. On the other hand, he supposed, it was probably no different to his endless talk about the merits of different stallions, and now it would just be her turn to have her own way. He only hoped that the play didn't run for ever.

After dinner they sat together on the sofa. Romantic pop music filled the room – some man groaning on about his matrimonial difficulties, no doubt to his accountant's intense satisfaction – and she stroked his head and gradually undressed him. His passion aroused, he clumsily but quickly removed her dress. She was naked underneath, save for her stockings and suspender belt, and he excitedly kissed and caressed her. Her cries of satisfaction reassured him that he could still arouse her, and the scratch marks on his back bore testimony to her ardour. All too soon it was over and she rolled off him on to the carpet. Reaching out for a cigarette from the packet on the table, she inhaled slowly and pensively as she stared up at the ceiling. He wondered what she was thinking, whether he really ever knew what was in her mind. Perhaps, he consoled himself, that was true of all marriages, but he only had his own to judge by. Outwardly their relationship was stable and secure, yet on occasions, particularly after they had made love, he wondered whether he understood Claudia at all, whether their life together was really one large compromise on her part and that as soon as the right moment arrived, she would weigh anchor and leave him. He dismissed the notion from his mind. Now that she had embarked on her career as an actress she would at long last find true fulfilment and that, he reasoned, could only be good for them both.

The ring of the phone made him start. 'I'll get it,' he said, but she appeared not even to have heard.

'Mr Rye?' The voice was unmistakable.

'What do you want?'

'Have you forgotten our little talk at the casino?'

'No, Mr Hassan, but . . .'

'Well? Have you anything to report?'

Morrow's message went through his mind but he had no desire to deliver it.

'I'm sorry, but Mr Morrow's been very busy, and anyway as I told you . . .'

'I don't care for your explanations. I will give you to the end of the month, Arc de Triomphe day, and then . . .'

The dead line said it all.

Chapter 5

Four weeks later, and with the Arc only five days away, there was still no news of Ramirez's whereabouts. Etienne Lafayette had been growing more hysterical by the hour and it had reached the stage that Alistair was pretending to be out when he called. Not surprisingly the Frenchman had lost all confidence in Ramirez's ability, and no doubt hoped that his next appearance would be on foreign soil. Morrow, on the other hand, remained confident.

'Look,' he said when Alistair went in to see him to suggest that Willie Grange should be given the ride, 'I've known this guy for years. He's a greedy son of a bitch and he won't throw up this opportunity of winning a big race. Anyway, he'll want to prove me wrong for getting rid of him.'

'Okay. If he likes money so much, how can you

explain his performance at Deauville? That was financial suicide.'

'I've been thinking about that, and do you know what I think? I think somebody paid him to take a pull.'

'You're joking. And you still want him to ride for you? Who do you think did it? Stride, I suppose?'

'More than likely. He'd only bought Rough Diamond the week before for what's rumoured to have been a small fortune, and what better way to ensure a proper return on your risk?'

'In other words, by cheating?'

'Alistair, there are times when I understand why you went bust. You've all the innocence of a hedgehog crossing a highway. It's time you joined the real world.'

Before Alistair could answer, the telephone rang.

'This won't take too long, it's my stockbroker. Fire away, Ivan. What's the price now? Up ten at seventy. Good. Keep on buying up to eighty-five, then I'll arrange a leak to the press that I'm the secret investor who's built up a stake. That'll worry the board and the price is bound to start motoring. As soon as everyone gets bid fever we'll sell out on the grounds of unwanted publicity.

Keep in touch.' He put down the receiver and grinned at Alistair.

'Don't look so shocked. Remember, it's greed and fear that motivate people and I trade in them just like any other commodity. When are you off to Paris?'

'I'm leaving on Thursday, meeting up at La Tremoille with Willie Grange and taking him down to Chantilly to ride out Philanderer early the next morning.'

'Are you taking Claudia over?'

''Fraid not. She's too busy rehearsing.'

'Shame. Take my advice: never come between a woman and her career. Look what happened to my first two wives. Thank God I no longer have to pay them alimony. I'm off to Chicago for the rest of the week and will meet you in Paris on Saturday. Come round to the Plaza and I'll buy you dinner.'

'And if Ramirez hasn't shown by then?'

'Your chum gets the ride. But don't worry. He will.'

It was only just daylight as Alistair and Willie left their hotel to drive to Chantilly. Even though he had had only four hours' sleep, Willie was in a very talkative mood and insisted on recounting the details of his recent amorous escapades. The subject eventually turned to Ramirez.

'There's a rumour going round that he was paid to pull Philanderer at Deauville. One or two of the French jocks were talking about it when they came over for that last Ascot meeting.'

'Did they say who put him up to it? Morrow suspects my old friend Stride. I suppose he's capable of it.'

'Easily. But this is the joke: the word is that both Stride and that Moroccan fellow, Hassan, paid him, and as you can imagine Hassan is not best pleased at being rolled over. No wonder the Mexican's keeping a low profile.'

By the time they had arrived at Etienne's stables the lads were busy saddling up the first lot of horses to be ridden out. They had just parked the car in the courtyard behind the trainer's house when he came running out brandishing a copy of *Paris Turf.*

'Thank God you've arrived! This is terrible, terrible! What will my owners think?'

'Hold on, Etienne, calm down. What's happened?'

'You mean you haven't heard? But it's all over *Paris Turf.* I never liked that man.'

'Which man, for God's sake?'

'Ramirez, who else? That treacherous bastard!'

'What's he done now?'

'Look!' Etienne handed Alistair the paper. 'He's gone and got himself murdered.'

'Meurtre Aux Courses', screamed the headline above an old photograph of Ramirez in Morrow's racing colours. Alistair's French was sufficient for him to pick up the important details: Ramirez's body had been found the day before in a disused cattle shed not far from the Honfleur to Lisieux road. The police, it claimed, believed that he had been dead for some weeks, but were refusing to give any more details. Alistair was stunned.

'But why?' he asked out loud, and immediately thought of Hassan and what Willie had just told him.

'How should I know?' said Etienne, shrugging his shoulders. 'It's typical of the man to let me down like this. This means the police will be all over my yard asking questions. I can't bear it. All I can tell them is that I hated the man and I haven't seen him since racing at Deauville. Like you.'

'Except I saw him at La Cage that evening.'

'So what? Two hours or so. What can it matter?'

A great deal, perhaps, thought Alistair to himself. 'At least our jockey problem has sorted itself out. Come on, Willie, you'd better get on with it. Can't keep Philanderer waiting, can we, Etienne?'

Willie changed quickly and was soon aboard the third favourite in the Arc betting. Alistair watched them leave the yard to make their way to the gallops, then headed for the phone in Etienne's study and the unenviable task of proving Morrow wrong, but not quite in the way he had anticipated. The number rang for some time before being answered.

'Yes? Wayne Morrow speaking.'

'Wayne, it's me, Alistair. I'm afraid I've got some bad news.'

'Not Philanderer?'

'No, the horse is fine. It's Ramirez. He's dead, murdered. His body's been found near Honfleur.'

'I don't believe it. Ramirez? Murdered? It can't be. Where are you now?'

'Down at Etienne's. He's throwing hysterics. No doubt the police will be over here to interview him and will also want to see you and me.'

'Try and calm him down. I'm leaving Paris on Monday so if the police want to see me it'll have to be tomorrow or early Sunday morning. Not that there's much I can tell them. I haven't seen Ramirez since the winners' enclosure at Deauville.

64

You can pass that on when you tell them about your last meeting.'

'Fine. I'll see you tomorrow, then.'

Alistair put down the receiver and stared out of the window at the stable yard which was now empty. 'Your last meeting,' he muttered to himself. Thank God he had Claudia as a witness. He decided to phone her later to refresh her memory.

Chapter 6

As always, the running of the Prix de L'Arc de Triomphe had attracted a huge crowd to Long-champs, and as with any great racing occasion, there was an exhilarating sense of excitement and expectation in the air. The horses had come from even further afield than the spectators, and of the eighteen declared runners three were from England, two from Ireland and one each from the United States, Australia and Japan. The first-prize money alone was in excess of 4,000,000 francs, making it the richest on offer in Europe, but that sum paled into insignificance compared with the potential increased stud value of any winning colt. The list of owners read like an anthology of the world's richest men, from Greek shipping magnates to Arab potentates. Amongst them were Morrow and Hassan, renewing their

Deauville rivalry. At least Alistair could console himself with the thought that Max Stride would not be in the winners' enclosure – Rough Diamond had injured himself in training and had been withdrawn earlier that week.

Etienne was in his usual state of high anxiety, although he had calmed down a little in comparison with the day before, when the police had visited the yard.

'They borrowed a photograph of you and Mr Morrow together with Ramirez,' he told Alistair as they walked towards the paddock after saddling up Philanderer.

'When was that taken?'

'After we won the Cork and Orrery at Ascot last year.'

'Did they say why they wanted it?'

'Not exactly, but they asked me who the people in the photograph were and when I told them, the inspector asked if they could borrow it. Of course I couldn't refuse.'

'I suspect it doesn't mean anything. Morrow and I may have been among the last to see him alive, and they'll want to eliminate us from their inquiries. Did they say how it was done?'

'No, they said nothing. Just asked questions about his money, his girlfriends, and whether I had any idea who might have done it. I told them everything I knew, and that in my opinion he was a very nasty man who was almost certainly mixed up with the underworld. I won't miss him. I just hope this English jockey of yours doesn't let us down. I would have preferred one of ours who knows the course.'

'Etienne, if the horse is good enough, the jockey is. He never let me down when I trained, and you seem to forget that it's my job that could be on the line if this goes wrong.'

They were only thirty-odd yards from the parade ring when Alistair spotted Hassan and his entourage directly ahead of them. In the drama of the last forty-eight hours he had forgotten that Hassan's ultimatum ran out that day and his instinctive reaction was to make an excuse to Etienne and head back towards the grandstand. Unfortunately it was too late. They had been spotted. Alistair could not avoid nodding his head in acknowledgement and just as they walked past the Moroccan party, he felt a tug on his sleeve which soon became an extremely painful clamp. He turned round to see Hassan pretending to smile but in reality giving him a highly menacing look through his tinted glasses.

'Monsieur Lafayette, will you spare your friend

for a few minutes? We have a little business to discuss.'

'Of course. Don't be too long, Alistair, they'll be bringing the horses into the paddock in a minute.'

Alistair decided to brazen it out. 'Yes, Mr Hassan, what can I do for you?'

'Don't play games. What is my answer?'

'I don't have one. With Ramirez's death it just hasn't been possible to discuss the matter properly with Mr Morrow. I need more time.'

'You have already had enough time. I can see that you don't take me seriously. I will give you one last chance. I will call you tonight at La Tremoille for my answer.'

'How did you know I was staying there?'

Hassan laughed. 'You are so innocent. I know where you stayed last night, where your wife stayed, even where your mother slept last night.'

'What the hell do you mean, bringing my wife and mother into this?'

'The choice is yours. Now go and see your beloved horse.'

The paddock was crammed with trainers, owners and jockeys exchanging last-minute instructions and hoping that in ten to fifteen minutes' time their optimism would have turned into reality. The great steward in the sky had ordained that the weather should be warm and sunny and the temperature remarkably high for early October. All the horses looked magnificent, the result of months of planning and training, their coats still retaining their summer sheen. In the middle of the paddock stood Morrow and Lafayette talking to Willie Grange; there was no doubt that the jockey was a good deal more relaxed than his trainer. Morrow was smoking a large cigar and appeared supremely unperturbed, as ever.

'Alistair, what's up?' asked Morrow. 'You look like you've seen a ghost.'

'Worse. I've just had an audience with Hassan.'

'Did you deliver my message?' the owner continued.

'Not exactly. He was more concerned with repeating his. We'll have to have a word about it later.'

'No need. I've got nothing more to say to that creep.'

Great, thought Alistair to himself. He just had time to wish Willie good luck when the announcement came for the jockeys to mount. There was to be a parade before the race, so Alistair decided to go and catch up on the latest betting news. He had never really adjusted to the idea of a racecourse without bookmakers, and marvelled at the

patience of the crowds as they queued in front of
the windows of the pari-mutuel, the French tote, to
put their money on. According to the television
monitors, Philanderer was third favourite, while
the French crowd had installed Hassan's horse as
an even-money shot. Boucher had recovered from
his Deauville injuries, his back being only badly
bruised and not broken as had originally been
feared.

Five minutes later the race was off and at a
cracking pace, considering the horses had a mile
and a half to run. The Japanese jockey seemed to
think there was a special prize for being first into
the home straight and was urging his mount on as
if the finishing post was already in sight. Philanderer had been badly drawn on the outside. Acting
on instructions, Willie had wisely settled him
down near the rear of the field and concentrated on
gradually working him over to a good position
about three places off the rails. Now it all depended on whether he had enough stamina and
finishing pace to come with a late run. As they
came round the final bend and into the straight
Philanderer was lying about tenth and the Japanese horse was going rapidly backwards. Seattle
Boy, the American challenger, had now come
through on the inside to take up the running, but

closing fast on his outside was the French Derby-winner Dehors. Willie had still not made a forward move and with only two furlongs to go, Alistair began to wonder whether he had taken the waiting game a little too seriously. The French crowd were now beginning to grow delirious and the roar grew as Maurice Boucher brought on Fille de Joie with a beautifully timed run on the outside. Seattle Boy was beginning to tie up on the rails as they passed the final furlong mark and it now looked as though the battle was between Fille de Joie, with Boucher driving like a man possessed, and Dehors on his inside nearer the rail. Gradually Fille de Joie forged half a length ahead but Alistair's binoculars were firmly fixed on Philanderer coming like a train on the wide outside in front of the grandstand. He was gaining on Fille de Joie with every yard and the only question was whether the winning post would come too soon. Willie was riding with all his strength, his head arched over Philanderer's neck as his whip repeatedly reminded the horse of the task before him. To the screams of the crowd they passed the post together and now it all hinged on the photograph.

Alistair and Morrow rushed down towards the winners' enclosure to hear Willie's verdict. They arrived just in time to see Maurice Boucher on

Fille de Joie being led into the winner's berth, to the great delight of her backers. Behind him and shaking his head anxiously at Etienne was Willie.

'I just don't know. It's bloody close,' was all he could say as he dismounted.

Etienne was beside himself with rage. 'Why did you come so late? *Mon Dieu*, why?'

He turned dejectedly towards Alistair and Morrow, in stark contrast to the whoops of elation coming from Hassan and his party.

'Well, Willie?' asked Morrow.

'I might have got up. He gave me a beautiful ride and one more stride and I'd have got past her.'

The wait seemed interminable, and Alistair could not bear to watch Hassan accepting congratulations as if the outcome was foregone. At last it came.

'*Résultat*,' boomed a voice over the loudspeaker and an expectant hush came over the crowd. '*Premier, numero quinze*, Philanderer.'

'We've won!' shouted Alistair. 'We've won!' He slapped Willie on the back and shook Morrow enthusiastically by the hand. Etienne went even further and gave Alistair a kiss.

'Exactly, Alistair: I was right. I told him to come with a late run.' The trainer now bubbled with enthusiasm himself.

Before Alistair could say anything he heard

someone call his name from the edge of the enclosure. He looked over to see two men, one in his late forties and the other about his own age.

'Monsieur Rye. May we have a word with you?'

'With me? If you're from the press we'll be holding a conference later.'

'No, Monsieur, we're from the Deauville police. I am Inspector Renard and this is my assistant Gilbert Tarot. We are investigating the murder of Jose Ramirez and must ask you to accompany us for questioning.'

'Do I have any choice?'

'To be honest, Monsieur, no.'

'I see.' Alistair turned to Morrow and told him what was happening.

Morrow was irate. 'What, now? They must be crazy.'

'There's nothing I can do. Just keep some champagne on ice for me tonight.'

'You bet. And don't take any crap from some guy playing at Maigret!'

Alistair looked at Inspector Renard. He could not have looked less like his image of the great French detective.

Chapter 7

The drive to Deauville took nearly three hours, with the speed limit being strictly observed on the motorway. The white police Peugeot was driven by a young gaunt-faced officer in uniform, with Tarot sitting beside him whilst Alistair and Renard sat in the back. Alistair's early attempts at conversation had met with polite *oui*s or *non*s and he soon gave up the effort. His own thoughts were hardly more encouraging. What should have been one of the most exciting days of his life was rapidly losing its allure. Of course, he reassured himself, he would be released once he told them about his meeting with Ramirez, and once they had telephoned Claudia to confirm his story. Presumably they would telephone and not send someone over there to question her. He just hoped that she hadn't gone out to lunch, or away for the day. At least he couldn't be a serious suspect. He had no criminal record and no reason to want Ramirez dead. Of course not, but then why were they taking him to Deauville to be questioned? They hadn't done that to Etienne, and they had made no attempt to question Morrow either, whom they must have recognised from the photograph. There was an uneasy sickly feeling in his stomach and he wished it would go away. He looked at the inspector, with his fat cheeks and unkempt beard. There was what looked like a piece of Brie clinging to the hair just below his mouth, no doubt a relic of his lunch on the way to Longchamps. Renard looked unwaveringly at the road ahead of them, now and again barking an instruction to the young driver and constantly puffing away at an endless succession of Turkish cigarettes.

Finally they arrived at the police station. They were obviously expected. Renard asked the officer on duty whether everything was ready. He then turned to Alistair.

'I spent two years on secondment with your Scotland Yard so my English is pretty good. Tarot here can't speak a word, so I will be carrying out the interview on my own. Before we start, there are one or two formalities to be completed and I would be grateful if you went with Tarot for a moment. Good.'

Alistair followed Tarot down a corridor and into a large room where another man, wearing a short white jacket, was waiting. He indicated to Alistair to roll up his sleeve and proceeded to take a sample of blood from his arm. That over, Tarot took his fingerprints and led him back along the corridor, up two flights of stairs and into another room. This one was empty except for a large square mahogany table in the middle, with a straight-backed chair on either side of it. Tarot said nothing and left.

The room was scarcely inspiring. The paint on the wall was peeling and the small window on the far side was barred. Somewhat incongruously, on the table stood a vase of flowers and even they looked like they were at the end of their life. It was only after he had looked round the room that Alistair noticed something else on the table, quite a large object wrapped up in a plastic bag. It seemed like an exhibit at a criminal trial or at least how such a thing would look on television. He walked over and looked at it more closely without picking it up. It was a knife, and he had an uneasy feeling that he had seen it somewhere before.

'Monsieur Rye.' The sound of the voice startled him and he whipped round to see Inspector Renard carrying a file and a notebook and at least two packets of cigarettes. 'I hope I didn't startle you.'

'No, Inspector. I was just looking at this knife.'

'Ah yes,' said Renard, picking it up in its bag. 'It is what the murderer used to kill Ramirez.'

It seemed to Alistair that the inspector gave him a knowing look but he had no intention of being compromised that easily.

'Really? Where did you find it?'

'About a mile and half from where we found the body. One of my men discovered it when searching the area. A bit of luck for us, and bad luck for the killer.'

'Yes. How can I help you, Inspector?'

'We shall soon find out. You, of course, knew the dead man well. Why not start by telling us everything you knew about him, and then perhaps about the last time you saw him alive?'

For over an hour Alistair told the history of his dealings with Ramirez, of his growing disenchantment with his riding, culminating in the disastrous race at Deauville.

'And so, Monsieur Morrow told you to dismiss him?'

'He did, and he came to see me on my instructions at our villa, or rather the one Mr Morrow had rented.'

'You mean La Cage, of course?'

'Yes, La Cage.' Alistair then told the inspector about the fight, how Ramirez had attacked him with the knife, and that since that evening he had neither seen, nor heard of, the Mexican.

'Of course,' he concluded, 'you can check all this with my wife. I'll give you our phone number in New York.'

'Of course, Monsieur, but first I have one or two small matters to discuss with you.'

'Fire away.'

'Good. After this fight you say you went out to dinner with some friends. Who were they? Please remind me?'

'The Donnellys.'

'Ah yes, and no doubt you told them about this frightening incident?'

'No, I didn't. Claudia, my wife that is, and I decided to tell nobody, not even my boss.'

'Isn't that a little strange? I mean, here you are attacked in your own home by a man with a knife who may kill you, and you tell nobody?'

'It might seem strange to you, but Mr Morrow doesn't like adverse publicity, and, well, I was worried he might think I was in some way to blame.'

'I'm sorry, forgive me, but how could you be to blame?'

'It's like this. My job was to tell Ramirez his retainer was not being renewed. It might be thought by his reaction that I had somehow provoked him, and anyway, Mr Morrow would scarcely be pleased with me if I went round

Deauville saying that I'd had a fight with his jockey. There's enough gossip around the place as it is.'

'What time did you say this fight took place?'

'He was meant to come at about 6.15, and I remember that he was surprisingly on time, give or take a few minutes. He said he was in a rush and had an appointment at 7.45 and . . .'

'An appointment? You didn't mention that before.'

'No, I'd forgotten all about that. I reckon the fight must have been at about 6.30 or so.'

'6.30. You're sure about that?'

'Not to the precise minute, but about then, yes.'

'You see, Mr Rye, we have reason to believe that Jose Ramirez was murdered at 6.35 that evening.'

'Don't be ridiculous, he can't have been. I – we – saw him leave La Cage alive then.'

'Would you be able to recognise Ramirez's watch?'

Alistair nodded. 'Yes, it was a gold Rolex. A present from Mr Morrow for winning the French Thousand Guineas. I think it was inscribed on the back.'

The inspector reached into his pocket and produced another plastic packet. He slowly removed its contents.

'Would this be the watch?'

'It looks very similar. Is there anything engraved on the back?'

'Yes. It says "To Jose Ramirez in gratitude", with a date after it.'

'That would be the date of the Thousand Guineas.'

'The face of this watch is broken. It has stopped at 6.35.'

'But that could be any day, surely.'

'Of course, but the date dial has also stopped at 31. And you see, Mr Ramirez did not die last week, on the 31st of September. We know that from our scientists, who have looked at his body, and not only because September has thirty days.'

Alistair could feel himself sweating. 'I didn't kill him. Why don't you phone my wife?'

'Please be patient. Of course we will phone her, but one or two more questions first. Do you recognise the knife here in this bag?'

'I'm not sure. Ramirez pulled it out while we were both on the floor. It all happened so quickly. It could be the one, I'm just not absolutely certain.'

'You see, this is the knife with which Ramirez was murdered and the only fingerprints on it are yours. Can you explain that?'

'Of course I can't. All I can tell you is that I wrestled it from his hand and picked it up off the floor to give back to him before making him leave.

Whoever murdered him has obviously removed their own fingerprints or was wearing gloves, and mine have been left on, I suppose.'

'And what about the traces of blood, your blood, which we have found under Ramirez's fingernails? How do you explain that? Something else the murderer left behind?'

'Don't be ridiculous. He scratched my face during the fight and some of the blood must have remained under his nails.'

'Just like the blood we found on the floorboards under the carpet at La Cage?'

Alistair hesitated. He couldn't remember any blood falling on to the floor but now he came to think about it there must have been some. 'No doubt that also came from our fight.'

'No doubt. Because you see, Mr Rye, this fight of yours is very convenient – you use it to explain the injuries to your face, your fingerprints on the knife, the blood on the carpet and so on. It is only the time on the watch which puts your little story in difficulties, but then no doubt you will say that it must have got broken also during the fight.'

Alistair decided that being cooperative was not getting him very far. 'I think I need a lawyer. Can I make a phone call?'

'Of course, in five minutes. We want you to stay here overnight whilst we continue our inquiries, so might I suggest you ask your lawyer to come here first thing tomorrow morning?'

'And my wife? When are you going to contact her? She'll confirm everything I've just told you.'

'But she would, wouldn't she?'

Alistair did not rise to the bait.

'Just one last question before I arrange for your supper and bed to be prepared. Perhaps you could think about it overnight.' The inspector paused to obtain the maximum effect. 'How long have you known that Ramirez was a heroin addict?'

Alistair was unable to locate Morrow at his hotel in Paris and left a brief message asking him to arrange for a lawyer to come to Deauville the following morning. He would have liked to have phoned Claudia, but Renard remained with him throughout and he certainly did not want to be accused of trying to rig her evidence. He was then given supper and shown to yet another room where he was to spend the night. This contained a single bed, a chair and a washbasin, and he had to submit to the ultimate indignity of having his tie taken away, no doubt in case he tried to commit suicide! It was quite clear that the police were now treating him as a serious suspect and he just wished that they would get on with it and speak to Claudia. After that he should be in the clear, but there was something disconcerting about Renard's attitude towards her evidence – as if it was to be distrusted because she was his wife. As he looked back on the interview and the questions he had been asked, it became obvious that he was the natural and easy suspect and that there was no incentive for the police even to look elsewhere. He had not said anything about Hassan, who, if Willie Grange was right, had every reason to want revenge on the jockey. And what about him being a heroin addict? That opened up a host of possibilities – a row with his supplier, another addict or possibly it was a gangland murder? Eventually he fell asleep, only to dream that he was on trial in a French court with Hassan as the judge and, even worse, Max Stride as the foreman of the jury.

He was still asleep when the door opened and a large, extremely well-built man carrying a dark blue attaché case was shown in by a uniformed policeman.

'Monsieur Rye? Let me introduce myself. I am Gaston Pression and I have been asked by Mr Morrow to represent you. We must get you out of here as quickly as possible.'

Alistair leapt from his bed and, feeling somewhat embarrassed, washed and dressed in front of the lawyer.

'How much do you know?' he asked anxiously.

'Only what Mr Morrow told me on the telephone last night. That a jockey has been murdered and that you have been brought here for questioning. The fact that they have kept you here overnight makes me think that it was more than just a routine interview.'

'You're right about that. That inspector there, Renard, thinks I killed Ramirez. So where would you like me to start?'

'At the beginning. Tell me everything you told the good inspector as well as anything else you now wish you had added.'

Alistair talked rapidly for the next half hour; Pression's only reaction was to grunt now and again or nod his head, and when Alistair had concluded there was a long pregnant silence.

'Well, Monsieur. It is obvious that you depend very much on the evidence of your wife. Without it, your story falls away and all the evidence points to you as the murderer.'

'You sound like you're on their side; I didn't kill him and my wife will back me up.'

'Your wife – she loves you?'

'Yes, of course.' Alistair was rather taken aback.

'Do you have a mistress perhaps, or does she have a lover?'

'No, neither, and I resent your suggestions.'

'Calm down. Remember I'm your lawyer. Unless

87

I know the complete story I cannot advise you properly. Here in France we expect people to have lovers, and with passion so often comes crime.'

'I'm sorry to disappoint you. We're just an old-fashioned monogamous union. When will the police talk to Claudia?'

'That's your wife? I expect they have already arranged for someone on the New York police to question her, but no doubt old Renard will take the opportunity of a free trip to America to investigate personally.'

'But they won't keep me locked up here till then, will they?'

'Oh no. What happens here in France is very different to England. The decision whether to investigate an individual further lies with an examining magistrate. He, or she, is normally quite young, at the beginning of their judicial career, and they decide whether there is enough evidence to prosecute and what investigations are necessary. The examining magistrate has complete control over investigations.'

'So when will he appear?'

'I have no doubt from what you say that Renard will hand the case over to him today. You will be interviewed again, but this time in my presence, and then released.'

'And that will be the end of it?'

'On the contrary. Just the beginning. The magistrate has wide powers and he will organise an investigation into your background, almost since you were a child.'

Alistair could not believe what he was hearing. 'But why don't they look for the real murderer?'

'They will, but we must face it that for the moment they think they have him already.'

'But what about all this heroin stuff? Surely that's a clue?'

'Very much so. They will investigate everything about Ramirez. You had no idea he was on drugs?'

'None. I had noticed he'd been behaving oddly but I never thought it could be that.'

'Is it possible he could be a carrier, a pusher?'

Alistair thought of Eddie James and his arrest for possession following York races, but dismissed it from his mind as coincidence. 'No, he earned enough as a jockey, I think.'

'No one ever is satisfied with what they earn. The police will undoubtedly make a search of his bank accounts and probably yours as well.'

'They won't have much luck there. As I told you, I was broke when I got my job with Morrow.'

They were interrupted by the appearance of Inspector Renard, who told them that Monsieur Boncuit, the examining magistrate, wished to see Alistair. And as the lawyer had predicted, Alistair had to retell his story which was then typed out to be signed. After some lengthy argument in French, Monsieur Pression secured his release from custody on the lawyer's undertaking that his client would report weekly to a police station wherever he was in France, and that he would return to assist in the forthcoming investigation whenever required. The expression on the examining magistrate's face (plainly a claret drinker, thought Alistair to himself) left them in no doubt that Alistair was still very much the number one suspect.

They drove back together to Paris in the lawyer's Citroen. His habit of taking his eyes off the road as he talked and gesticulated to Alistair didn't help his passenger's nerves.

'Presumably they would never charge me if Claudia backs me up?' Alistair ventured.

'On the contrary. There is nothing a lawyer enjoys tackling more in front of a jury than the alibi *passionnel. Mon vieux,* I must warn you – your troubles are only just beginning.'

Chapter 8

Alistair took the first plane home to New York, arriving there just after five o'clock in the afternoon. As he went through customs he was stopped and his suitcase thoroughly searched. It was the first time that had ever happened and he could not believe it was just coincidence. There was something about the way he had been singled out by the customs officer, to the exclusion of any other passenger, which made him both suspicious and uneasy. Almost immediately the officer had been joined by a colleague and the more Alistair tried to appear relaxed when answering their questions, the more he could feel the sweat itching on his brow. Even when he walked purposefully away from them to the exit, he still felt that they were following him with their eyes.

To his relief, Claudia was there to meet him. She

had not been home when he called from Paris, so he had only been able to leave a message on the answerphone. The red marks which circled her eyes showed that she had been crying, and as she threw her arms around him she was clearly distressed.

'Alistair, thank God you're back. It's been terrible.'

'Darling, I'm so sorry. Just try and calm down and tell me what's happened.'

'Last night about eight o'clock two men came to the apartment. They weren't wearing uniforms or anything. They said they were police officers and that they wanted to talk to me urgently about you.'

'Did you let them in? You didn't have to.'

'I didn't think about that at the time. I thought you might've been involved in some accident or something, and once I'd seen their identity badges I let them in. They then told me that you were being questioned by the French police about Ramirez's murder and that, as he was an American citizen, they were pursuing their own inquiries in New York.'

'Hold on. Let's grab a cab and you can tell me the rest on the way home.'

Five minutes later they were on their way to their apartment and Claudia continued her story.

'They asked what I knew about Ramirez and lots of questions about your job and your trips to Europe. And then they asked about the last time we'd seen him alive, so I told them about the evening at La Cage. Just like we discussed it on the phone on Saturday. Oh Alistair, I'm afraid. They were so persistent, wanting every little detail. They don't really suspect you, do they?'

'If they don't, they're putting on a pretty good act. The inspector who questioned me is behaving like I'm the one and only suspect.'

'But that's ridiculous. We both saw Ramirez leave La Cage after the fight.'

'I know that, but unfortunately we appear to be the last people to have seen him alive. They've found the murder weapon, or so they claim, and it just happens to be the knife he pulled on me, with my fingerprints all over it.'

'But what about the fight? That explains it all, doesn't it?'

'They just say I've made it all up to cover up for the blood on the carpet and the traces of my blood they found under his fingernails.'

'Oh my God, but it's ridiculous! Why would you want to kill him?'

'They're still working on a motive. The final shock came when they announced that Ramirez was a heroin addict. The lawyer Wayne hired for me suspects that they're going to try and link me to his drug taking, too.'

'Won't the autopsy establish the time of death?'

'Even better. They've got his watch which was broken at 6.35 on the 31st and they say that shows he was murdered at that time on the last day of August.'

'But that's when he was at La . . .'

'Exactly. All very neat.'

'But they're not going to charge you, or anything, are they?'

'Not yet. Hopefully when they hear what you've told the police over here they'll begin to believe my story, but I don't reckon that French inspector is going to give in too lightly. From now on I'm under suspicion until the real murderer is caught.'

'And when will that be?'

'Your guess is as good as mine. In the meantime I've absolutely no intention of sitting on my backside and waiting for Inspector Renard to slip a pair of handcuffs on me. Willie Grange told me one or two interesting things over in France about our friend Ramirez and when I'm in England for the sales I might do a bit of investigating on my own.'

'Is that safe?'

'Almost certainly not, but I haven't come this far to give it all up again. Don't worry, we're a long way off standing in the dock together yet.'

'Together? Alistair, what d'you mean?'

'I'm only joking! But don't you see, if I murdered Ramirez that evening, what were you doing at the time?'

The cab drew up outside their apartment block before Claudia had a chance to say anything else. Alistair went into their bedroom to unpack and noticed that somebody had been through his wardrobe.

'Claudia? Did you let the police search through my things?'

'I'm sorry, I forgot to tell you. They asked if they could see the suit you were wearing the night Ramirez visited La Cage. It was that light blue one you always wear in the summer, so I showed it to them and then they asked if they could take it away.'

'Did they say why?'

'No. I'm sorry, I was so confused I just didn't think. I can't believe it's of any importance. It's been to the cleaners since we got back, anyway.'

Alistair remembered there had been some blood on the sleeve of the jacket but he hadn't checked to see whether the stains had come out after cleaning. He resolved to say nothing to Claudia and to continue unpacking. He'd just finished when the phone rang. It was Wayne.

'Hi! Are you all right? You had me scared with that message last night at the hotel.'

'Well, I'm here and still alive, but that's about all. Are you staying at the office? Good. I'll come in and give you the lowdown. I only hope you've got nothing against murder suspects.'

Morrow seemed horrified as Alistair recounted what had happened at the police station.

'Why didn't you tell me that Ramirez had attacked you? After that there would've been no way that I'd have let him ride for me again.'

'I knew you'd think that, but Claudia and I discussed it and we were afraid that you might think I'd mishandled the situation.'

'But that's ridiculous. And I suppose the fight explains the cut to your eye and the scratch marks on your face when you came back to New York?'

'One and the same. I'm just sorry that I sort of lied to you.'

'That doesn't bother me, but if you'd only told me when I phoned from Paris that night, it would've made things a whole lot easier. Would it help if I told the police that you did tell me about the fight when I called?'

'It's a nice thought, but no thanks. I've done nothing wrong and I've told the police the whole truth. I just hope once they've seen Claudia for themselves the French police will get off my back. What do you think about Ramirez being on heroin?'

Morrow shook his head. 'I can't believe it. Why would he need to? After all, I paid him a fortune.'

'That was my reaction. Do you think I should've told them about that English jockey being arrested with the stuff?'

'Why should you? There can't be any connection, can there?'

'That's what I thought, but we were at York races the day he was caught. I thought it might be worth following up; you never know, it might lead somewhere.'

'That's up to you. But keep my name out of it. Drugs are one thing I can do without.'

'Promise, and thanks for that lawyer. He's not exactly a laugh a minute, but he strikes me as a cunning old bugger.'

'That's what you need. He's the partner of a man who does a lot of work for me in France. I'm told he specialises in big criminal trials.'

'I'm glad to hear it. I just hope that yours truly isn't going to be in one of them.'

Morrow laughed. 'A true Englishman. Never loses his sense of humour. How about a drink? We haven't celebrated Sunday's great win yet.'

'Good idea.'

Five minutes later they were toasting Philanderer over a couple of large martinis, followed by another couple and another couple. For the first

97

time in twenty-four hours Alistair felt genuinely relaxed. Morrow was now in high spirits and with the air of a caring father he put his arm round his racing manager.

'Don't worry. Everything's going to be fine. The French police will get the true villains and soon all this business will be forgotten. Here's another toast.' He lifted his glass dramatically and a little unsteadily into the air. 'To justice.'

The very thought made Alistair uneasy.

Chapter 9

The next day Alistair left for England and the Newmarket sales. The annual auction of yearlings had always been one of his favourite times in the year, when owners, trainers, agents and breeders took part in a frenzied redistribution of wealth. Unquenchable optimism reverberated around the bars and restaurants, fired by glass after glass of champagne. The very rich, clustered by their advisers and trainers, gathered to bid against each other in the search for the super horse, the colt who would go on to win the Derby and earn millions at stud, or the filly which would triumph in the Thousand Guineas or Oaks and become the broodmare of the century. The fact that there could be only one Derby winner a year was irrelevant – however distant the dream, that it was even capable of realisation was enough.

It was sometimes hard to understand how so much money could be spent by so many different people, but every year the number of horses in training increased. It was fortunate for breeders and bookmakers alike that there was ultimately no science to the creation of a winner. Happily, fate and nature had conspired to make even the best-bred horses on occasions pedestrian, with horses costing in their millions running not much faster than an enthusiastic show pony, while others, of more unorthodox pedigree, run as if their very lives depend on it – which suggests that they have brains as well!

Morrow had told Alistair that he could spend up to £10,000,000 in buying fifteen yearlings, and he could not help but feel excited at the prospect of going to Newmarket with spending-power equal to almost anyone else there. What was more, he regarded it as a further affirmation of Morrow's trust in his judgement, possibly one step nearer the day when he would set him up as one of his trainers. He made up his mind to forget about the events in France for that week and to concentrate, with the assistance of Jack Donnelly, on searching out likely candidates for Morrow's funds. Fortunately no one other than Morrow and Claudia knew about his role in the Ramirez murder inquiry, and he just hoped that for once the normal cyclone of rumours which sweeps around race-courses had not brought this particular piece of news from France. Early references to Ramirez by other visitors to the sales enabled him to feel more relaxed – the Mexican jockey appeared to have been universally disliked and there was a marked lack of interest in the identity of his murderer. He just hoped that state of affairs would continue.

Together, he and Jack spent Thursday morning looking over a selection of yearlings, who on their breeding alone were classified as high-flyers. Auctioneers understandably never indulge in anything so cautious as restrained optimism. One particular lot, to be sold that evening, had captured their attention, a bay colt by Nijinsky out of a Classic-winning mare. The broad grin on the Irish breeder's face made it clear that intense interest had already been shown in his creation and Alistair was under no illusion that the bidding would be anything but high and competitive.

'Who else has looked at him?' he asked the breeder casually, trying not to give away his own enthusiasm. The small impish-faced man hesitated before replying as he scratched his head.

'Let me think now. Oh yes, there was one or two of those Arab princes and that Moroccan fellow, Hassan, isn't it?'

Alistair merely nodded. He knew that Hassan

would be at the sales, but he had hoped that he would be able, with the help of Jack Donnelly, to avoid any direct personal contact.

Returning to his hotel for lunch, he telephoned Morrow to obtain specific instructions as to his limit for the Nijinsky colt. Morrow's reaction on hearing that Hassan was a potential rival was just as he had expected.

It was just after nine o'clock when lot 136 entered the sales ring. Alistair and Jack had decided not to sit down but to stand at the back to the right of the auctioneer. From that position they had a good view of all the other bidders. Alistair could see Hassan standing almost directly opposite him on the other side, no doubt adopting a similar tactic. As usual he was surrounded by his team of hand-picked granite-faced heavyweights. The bidding opened at 100,000 guineas and moved rapidly to 500,000. So far, bloodstock prices that year had shown that this was the level when the men were separated from the boys, in terms of buying power.

'At 600,000 guineas,' shouted the auctioneer. The bid was Hassan's.

'650,000.' This time the bidder was a bloodstock agent acting for a well-known American millionaire sitting in the very front row.

Hassan was not to be outdone and signalled with his catalogue.

'700,000 guineas on my left,' shouted the auctioneer. 'Come along, gentlemen, please. You're not going to let this beautifully bred colt go so cheaply, I hope.'

Plainly the bloodstock agent agreed with him and immediately increased his bid.

'I have 800,000 guineas from the front row.'

Hassan waved his catalogue again.

'900,000 on my left.' He looked down at the agent.

'A million over here in front of me.'

Alistair could now sense the change in atmosphere in the sale ring. There was nothing so fascinating as watching people spend fortunes at an auction, and the bidding had now reached a level where the non-bidders stopped talking and started watching the rivalry develop.

'1,100,000,' the auctioneer shouted, having taken another bid from Hassan. He looked down from his rostrum expectantly towards the bloodstock agent. There was no response, no waving of a hand or catalogue. He, or more accurately his client, had had enough. Alistair looked over at Hassan. In the glare of the light he could see a complacent grin coming over the Moroccan's face as he thought that he had won.

'On my left at 1,100,000 guineas. Gentlemen, do you really want to let this magnificent-looking animal go at this price? Who will bid me 1,200,000? Do I hear one million two?'

He looked around the sale ring, and as he did so Alistair caught his eye and lifted the index finger of his right hand.

'Thank you, sir. I'm bid one million two on my right.'

Hassan wasted no time and waved his catalogue.

'One million three,' shouted the auctioneer.

Alistair raised his finger again.

'One million four,' shrieked the auctioneer.

Hassan responded immediately and within seconds the bidding had reached the two million mark, easily a record for the sales so far. The last bid had been Alistair's and now all eyes turned on the Moroccan to see if he had the nerve or the desire to continue.

The auctioneer egged him on. 'You've come this far, sir; one more bid may well secure him.'

Alistair wondered whether Hassan could understand a word. He seemed more intent on staring poisonously over at his rival.

He lifted his catalogue.

'Thank you, sir, you won't regret it, I'm sure. 2,100,000 guineas on my left.'

It was now Alistair's turn to be the focus of attention. Jack Donnelly was tugging anxiously at his sleeve.

'That's enough, Alistair. Let him have it. If you go any further, Morrow will go through the roof!'

Alistair lifted his finger again.

'2,200,000!' yelped the auctioneer with unconcealed delight.

'Christ!' muttered Donnelly.

Hassan's reaction was instantaneous.

'2,300,000,' bayed the auctioneer, no doubt mentally calculating the commission.

Alistair didn't flinch.

'2,400,000,' roared the auctioneer, his enthusiastic tone in sharp contrast to the language which Donnelly was now using.

Now Hassan hesitated. Alistair suspected that he had already bid far more than he had intended, driven on by his hatred of Morrow and refusal to admit defeat. This time he did not lift his catalogue but merely mouthed something to the auctioneer.

'I'm bid 2,500,000 guineas. On my left, 2,500,000 guineas.' You could tell that he got extra pleasure from rolling those words around his lips. He was almost salivating with delight.

It was Alistair's turn to go quiet. He could feel a thousand eyes looking at him and he could hear

Jack Donnelly begging him to give up. He certainly couldn't afford a repeat of the Stride fiasco – an unauthorised bid.

The auctioneer looked at him hopefully. He too must have suspected that Alistair had reached his limit.

'On my left, then, at 2,500,000 guineas. Have you all done, gentlemen? This magnificent colt, going once, going twice . . .' He hesitated and looked for the last time around the ring. Hassan was now grinning again at the thought of his victory.

Alistair slowly and deliberately lifted his finger.

'On my right at 2,600,000!' sang the auctioneer, turning at once towards Hassan. But this time all he could see was the Moroccan's back as he stormed out of the sales ring.

'Jesus! Alistair, what the hell have you gone and done?' cried Jack. 'The old man's going to murder you!'

'Aren't you pleased?' replied Alistair. 'You said this morning he was the best-looking colt here and cheap at any price. You're not saying you've changed your mind?' He was pretending to be angry.

'I know I did, but 2,600,000! And guineas as well. That's a hell of a lot of money.'

'Don't tell me! I'd better go and phone Morrow.'

'Won't he go through the roof?'

'Jack, I'm not that silly. I'm not going to be accused of making the same mistake twice. I telephoned from the hotel after lunch and he told me I could bid up to 2,500,000, plus one.'

'You mean that was your last bid?'

'Dead right it was. I just gambled on Hassan having a limit, even against me and Morrow, of two and a half. Let's just hope that the horse's worth it or Hassan will have the last laugh. Shall we go and have a bottle?'

'One bottle? You've got to be joking! I'm going to get well and truly plastered tonight!'

'That shouldn't be very difficult; there'll be a queue of hopeful trainers at the bar waiting to treat us.'

'Let's not keep them waiting, then!'

It was well past two o'clock when Alistair and Jack returned to their hotel and made their way unsteadily to their respective rooms. Jack insisted on taking the lift while Alistair preferred to struggle up two flights of stairs. They had drunk endless bottles of champagne and had managed to destroy the calm of one of the restaurants in the middle of the town. Jack had told story after story, confirming that he hadn't just kissed the Blarney stone, but made love to it. Alistair used the corridor wall

to guide him in the darkness to room 208. Opening
the door he reached out to the wall on his left and
felt clumsily for the light switch. Instead of wallpaper his hand found a prickly uneven surface
which felt unmistakably like someone's chin. He
had no time to react. A hand grabbed his collar,
throwing him across the room, and at the same
time the door was shut behind him.

'Welcome home, Mr Rye. I hope you had a good
evening.' The voice was all too familiar.

'Very nice up to now, but I would prefer not to
talk to you in the dark, Mr Hassan.'

The Moroccan laughed, but it sounded more like
a dog howling at the moon.

'Turn on the light,' he barked, and immediately
his order was obeyed. For a moment Alistair was
dazzled, but even through his alcoholic stupor he
could count three visitors: Hassan was sitting in
the armchair by the window; and on either side of
the door stood a member of his supporters' club.
They looked even more vicious than usual and
would have fitted most of the identikit pictures
issued by the police. Alistair waited for Hassan to
talk. Clearly this was not intended to be a social
visit.

'Mr Rye. I'm very distressed by your attitude,
which I must assume is also the attitude of your
employer. In the last few weeks it has become

obvious that you do not take my warnings seriously. And now this evening you again humiliate
me.'

Alistair couldn't think of anything to say. Hassan had never appeared very interested in his side
of the story and the presence of the heavy mob
didn't indicate a change of approach.

'I note your silence. I think it is sensible. The
time has come for me to show you that I like to be
taken seriously. Abdul.' The next sentence was
incomprehensible and Alistair assumed it was in
Moroccan. Its impact was immediate. One of the
heavyweights grabbed him and held his left hand
behind his back in a half-nelson, using enough
force to make Alistair feel his arm would break at
any moment.

'What the hell are you playing at?' he shouted.
The response was for his attacker to put his free
arm over Alistair's mouth. The other now moved
forward. Alistair watched in disbelief as he drew a
pair of pliers out of his pocket and holding them in
his right hand grabbed Alistair's right arm and
jerked it forward with the palm facing downwards.
Hassan spoke in Moroccan again, sneering all the
while at Alistair and clearly enjoying every moment of his victim's discomfort. Whatever he said,
it plainly excited his underlings. Alistair now
watched in dismay as, at Hassan's direction, the

jaws of the pliers were clamped on to the end of the fingernail of his index finger – the self-same finger which only five hours before had been lifted in triumph. Gradually and agonisingly the pressure of the pliers was applied, as if the removal of every centimetre of nail from its roots was to be savoured. The pain was soon unbearable, but Hassan had no intention of stopping there. He beckoned to his henchmen to lift Alistair to his feet and hold him by either arm. Then, with a look of undiluted pleasure on his face, he took Alistair's finger in his mouth and bit on it through the skin until the blood dripped from his lips. Alistair lost consciousness just as the macabre silence was broken by the sound of the bone breaking.

Chapter 10

The prolonged ringing of the phone woke him up. He was lying fully dressed across the bed, just where they had abandoned him in the early hours of the morning. His whole finger was throbbing and it was accompanied by a nagging rhythmic pounding inside his head, a reminder of his drinking session with Jack Donnelly. He was tempted not to answer, to let the world sort out its own problems for the day, but when the caller showed no signs of giving up he relented. It was Maître Pression.

'Monsieur Rye, so you are there? I was beginning to give up.'

'I'm sorry. I had a heavy night last night. What time is it, by the way?'

'Here in Paris it is nine o'clock, which means eight o'clock over there in England. Your wife told

me to ring early to be sure I caught you before you
went out inspecting horses.'

'When did you speak to her?'

'Last night, which would have been in the
afternoon her time. I'm sorry to disturb you, but
I'm afraid it's important.'

'What's happened?'

'I had a call yesterday morning from the examining magistrate. He's a very arrogant man, but
there's no point in upsetting him. He tells me that
they've obtained inspection of Ramirez's bank accounts, revealing the receipt over the last year of
substantial sums of cash. He wants you to provide
details of all payments which you have made to
him as a jockey.'

'I can do that, but naturally I'll have to discuss it
first with Mr Morrow.'

'Of course. No problem. What's more, he'd like to
see copies of your bank statements over the last
year. Strictly speaking, he's no jurisdiction over
English banks but he can always ask the help of
the English police and non-cooperation on your
part might look – how would you say? – suspicious.'

'I see. I'd like to think about that. Why do they
want them, anyway?'

'The magistrate was not very forthcoming but I
gathered they're now working on the theory that

Ramirez was a drug smuggler. He said something about an English jockey who has been arrested and there could be a possible link.'

'But how could that involve me?'

'This will sound ridiculous. They think that you may somehow be part of the gang. Of course I just laughed at the suggestion, but once they've an idea in their little heads, nothing can dislodge it.'

'Did the magistrate have anything else to say? Like trying to find Ramirez's killer instead of hounding an innocent person like me?'

'Please don't get so worked up. In fact, I believe Inspector Renard is going to New York to interview your wife. She made a rather bad impression on the American police and so our dear inspector wants to go over there to see her for himself.'

'That's ridiculous. She's been scared enough as it is, with police bursting into our flat and taking away my clothing. I'm going to get a lawyer over there to be present if he tries to see her. Is there anything else to tell me, like some good news for once?'

'One last thing, but I wouldn't describe it as exactly good. I understand the police in New York removed the suit you were wearing the last time you saw Ramirez?'

'They had no right to do that.'

113

'I agree, but it's too late to complain now. It appears that there are bloodstains on the sleeve and that these match Ramirez's blood group.'

'So what? I told you; I cut his lip in the fight and some blood must have splattered over me. It's all consistent with my story.'

'I know that, it's just that the police here are looking at it from the other perspective.'

'What other perspective?'

'You know very well. We discussed this in the car on the way to Paris.'

'Remind me.'

'That you murdered Ramirez, and have invented this story of the fight to explain the evidence against you.'

'That's a lie. I thought everyone was presumed innocent until they were proven guilty, or doesn't that apply in France?'

'A noble sentiment. Alas, in my experience it's all too often the other way round.'

'Thanks very much. At this rate I may have to do a little detective work myself.'

'I cannot stop you, but please be careful.'

Alistair looked down at the naked skin on his broken finger. 'Don't worry. From now on I have every intention of being so.'

His first step was to phone Willie Grange at his flat

in Newmarket and ask him to come over. Luckily the jockey was not riding that day, and twenty minutes later he was sitting in the chair that had been occupied by Hassan only a few hours earlier. Alistair had used the time to bath and shave and to put a plaster on his finger. Owing to his clumsiness with a razor he always kept a ready supply. Willie was indignant when he heard about Hassan's escapade.

'The bastard. I've only ridden for him once and he spent the whole time telling me what to do. I bet the fat slob never sat on a horse in his life. Do you want me to get some of the lads to work him over?'

'No thanks. I've got enough difficulties without taking the law into my own hands, at least not that way.' In fact Alistair was uncertain just who the lads were. Willie often referred to these mythical figures whenever he felt an injustice had been committed and instant retribution was called for.

'It wasn't about Hassan I wanted to talk to you. I haven't told you what happened last Sunday after the Arc when those two policemen took me away.'

'I gathered from Etienne that you were being interviewed about Ramirez. He said it was nothing to worry about, just the police being a little dramatic.'

'I wish it were that simple. The inspector who questioned me is trying to suggest that I killed

115

Ramirez when he came to see me after the Deauville race.'

'But that's a joke! You couldn't hurt a fly; in fact that's always been your problem. If you'd allowed me to have got the lads in, Stride would've paid up without a murmur. Why would you want to kill Ramirez, anyway?'

'They haven't suggested a motive yet, but I've got a nasty feeling – and so has my French lawyer – that one's on its way.'

'And what's that? Don't tell me – because he didn't ride to instructions?'

'Willie, this isn't a joking matter. Had you ever heard that Ramirez was a heroin addict?'

'Now it's you who's joking. An addict? You don't mean he used to inject himself with the stuff? Christ, I lent him my towel once at the races.'

'Don't worry, it's not contagious! Do you think there could be any connection between him and Eddie James?'

'What d'you mean?'

'Well, you know, Ramirez was at York races the day Eddie was caught, and there would be nothing easier than for a jockey like Ramirez, who's travelling round Europe to different race tracks, to add a few grams of heroin to his travelling kit.'

'Dead simple, come to think of it. I've never been

searched at customs over the last five years, that's when there is any customs at those small airfields. But where do you fit in to all this?'

'As yet I'm not quite sure. Suppose the police say Ramirez was just the carrier. Their next stop is to find the supplier, the Mister Big you always read about in the papers, living in luxury somewhere on the Continent.'

'You? That's ridiculous.'

'You know that and I know that; the trouble is whether the French police will believe it. And that leads me on to the next problem which, I'm afraid, involves you.'

'Me? How come? You don't want me to confess, do you?'

'You'll stop joking when you hear this. The French police have discovered large cash receipts in Ramirez's bank account which they think are evidence he's been up to no good. Some of them I can explain, although that's going to cause someone else a good deal of embarrassment. They now want access to my accounts over here in England.'

'So what's the problem? There's no crime in being broke, is there?'

'That's not the point. Thanks to your tips over the last season I've paid about thirty thousand quid in cash into my account.'

117

'Bloody hell! I didn't know you were punting that heavily.'

'I just took the risks and they came off. I also knew that you happened to be one of the few jockeys who can actually spot a good thing when you see it. Thanks to your tips I've been able to pay off the last of my debts to the bank.'

'I still don't see the problem.'

'Willie, I adore you! That's either because you're stupid or just bloody naive. Jockeys aren't allowed to pass on information, remember, and if I tell the police about our little association, Willie Grange will end up in front of the stewards and bang goes your licence and your job with Toby Hartley.'

'Oh.' Willie's complexion lost its usual rosy colour as he grasped the implications of what Alistair had said. 'I've got you now. Yes, this could be difficult.' For once Alistair noticed there was no mention of the lads.

'This French lawyer fellow.'

'Maître Pression.'

'Whatever. Is he any good? Can't he tell the French Bill to mind their own business and get on with finding the real villains?'

'I think he's good. Morrow uses his partner the whole time, and happily for me is picking up the bill. What he says is that it's in my interest to be cooperative, and once the police realise that

Claudia and I are telling the truth, they'll leave me alone and look elsewhere.'

'Did you tell them about Hassan, and what I told you on the way to Chantilly that morning? I mean, he's just the sort to rub out Ramirez for cheating him. Wouldn't even give him indigestion after his couscous or whatever it is those people eat.'

'No, I deliberately didn't say anything about him. All you knew was based on rumour and the last thing I wanted to do was make false allegations against that madman. If he rips my finger-nail out for outbidding him, how do you think he'd treat the odd allegation of murder?'

Willie didn't reply but merely got up from his chair and walked over and kicked the end of the bed in exasperation.

'What you need, you know, is a lawyer, not one of these Frogs, but an English one who can tell you what to do.'

'Who do you suggest? The only ones I know are in the sticks, and spend their lives drawing up wills or conveyances. I doubt whether there are any precedents for heroin-smuggling and murder inquiries.'

'I've got an idea. James Thackeray, who writes on the *Sportsman*, was in a spot of bother last year over the Croft murder. He's bound to know somebody. Can I use the phone?'

119

Willie located Thackeray at his flat and was given the number of a firm of solicitors in Lincoln's Inn.

He handed Alistair the receiver. 'Here we are. He says some chap called Fergus Pollock seemed to know a lot about crime when he met him. All the other lawyers he knows are either too expensive, or in their eighties, or both.'

As Alistair dialled the number, he imagined his finger was in Hassan's eye, poking the jelly-like cornea to the screams of the Moroccan. Sadism wasn't one of his vices, but he was beginning to nurture a desire for physical revenge on the Moroccan, a sensation he had never experienced before.

Fergus Pollock was in, but as he explained to Alistair, already engaged on a long and bitterly contested fraud case at the Old Bailey. He suggested that Alistair come up to London that morning and see one of his partners, Amy Frost. Somewhat reluctantly, Alistair agreed. There was no problem leaving that day's bidding in the capable if somewhat shaky hands of Jack Donnelly. What worried him was the idea of a dowdy woman lawyer advising him to be patient and trust to justice. In his present state that would be about as reassuring as telling a drowning man to keep calm because you've sent for a pair of flippers.

Chapter 11

The offices of Arthurs, solicitors, were tucked away in the corner of Lincoln's Inn. Alistair had never been to this part of London before, just north of the Strand behind the Law Courts, and he found it hard to believe that such a peaceful and rural setting, with its Queen Anne buildings, could still exist in the heart of the metropolis. The black iron plate at the entrance to their building proclaimed that Arthurs were also Commissioners for Oaths, and he chuckled at the idea of people calling in off the streets to let off a few swear words for a couple of quid and then returning to normal life. The stairs had been worn down by the heavy tread of anxious litigants. Alistair sat down on a dilapidated sofa and pretended to read a two-year-old copy of *Country Life* devoted to Cruft's dog show. As he waited for Miss Frost to get rid of her

121

previous client he couldn't help listening in to the receptionist's call. The girl was busily engaged in what sounded like a conversation with one of her girlfriends; it seemed that her boyfriend had started taking liberties at the cinema the night before and she was now torn between giving him the push or going to bed with him. Lucky old him, he thought to himself, if that was his only problem in life! He began to wonder what Miss Frost would look like. The name conjured up an image of a prim, bespectacled spinster, probably in her late forties, who took life extremely seriously and did not know the first thing about racing. The best he could hope for was a bluestocking, or more likely blue tights, who had a boyfriend called Charles and drove a Volkswagen Golf which Daddy had given her for passing her solicitor's exams. He was miles away in his thoughts when he heard his name being called. He looked up to see an extremely attractive dark-haired girl, about five foot seven, wearing a rather elegant dark blue suit. Her narrow waist was at his eye level and he felt an immediate and almost irresistible desire to grab her.

'Mr Rye? Please come this way.'

With pleasure, he said to himself, as he followed her up another flight of stairs and into a bright office on the floor above. If Miss Frost was half as attractive as the girl he took to be her secretary, things were beginning to look up. She closed the door behind them and held out her hand.

'Hello, I'm Amy Frost. Please sit down and tell me how I can help you.'

'You're Amy Frost?'

'One and the same. Fergus Pollock told me that you're in some kind of difficulty, drugs or something, and you needed advice urgently. You'd better tell me all about it.'

Alistair looked round the room whilst he collected his thoughts. The *Sporting Life* calendar on the wall behind Miss Frost's desk was a hopeful sign.

'You don't like horse racing, by any chance?'

'I love it. My father and brother ride in point to points and I've been brought up in a household where if you didn't want to talk about racing you might as well join a nunnery. Personally I prefer the flat. I find the form more dependable when it comes to having a bet.'

'Really?' Alistair couldn't believe his luck. 'I used to be a trainer.'

'Of course. Now it all makes sense. Fergus said you had something to do with racing. You must be the Alistair Rye who used to train at Newmarket.'

123

It was now Alistair's turn to say, 'One and the same.'

'But why did you give it up? You were doing really well, particularly with sprinters, if my memory's right.'

'It gave me up. I misjudged one of my owners and as a result lost rather a lot of money. Anyway, that's yesterday's bad news. I'd better tell you about my present problems.'

For the next hour Alistair recounted the events which had led him to her office. Feeling that a touch of female sympathy wouldn't do him any harm, he told her about Hassan and his revenge over the auction.

'So now, you see, things are looking pretty bad for me every way I turn. What I'd like to find out is what's happened to Eddie James and whether there really is anything in this drug business. I'd also like your advice on whether I should give the police access to my bank account. Can I stop them telling Willie Grange's boss or the Jockey Club about all the information he's passed on to me? The last thing I want to do is ruin his career.'

'As to Eddie James, I'll phone a friend of mine on the drugs squad and ask him off the record what's happening. Hold on, and I'll ask Sheila on reception to get the number for me.'

It took a couple of minutes for Sheila to stop

talking about her boyfriend before Amy could give her the number she wanted.

'As to the bank account, I think we ought to have a word with your bank manager and see if any official request has yet been made to him. They love doing all these things properly, you know. Give me his number, and we can talk to him after I've spoken to my friend at the Yard.'

'Do you think the French police have a case against me?'

'Not so long as your wife continues to corroborate you. She will, won't she?'

'Oh yes. I mean, there's no problem there. We're happily married and all that. Anyway, she's no reason to lie.'

'In that case, even if they charge you, you're sure to be acquitted. There's nothing that can connect you to this drug business, is there? If there is, now's the time to come clean.'

'Nothing, I swear to you, but recently things have had a nasty habit of turning up to my detriment.'

At that moment Amy's call came through from the Yard. Alistair couldn't help but admire the way she turned on the charm to dig out information 'off the record' from the officer on the case. She finished the conversation with a promise to buy him lunch.

125

'It's quite interesting. The police say they're convinced they're on to something big and that James is part of a large drug-smuggling racket bringing heroin and cocaine into this country. He's been very uncooperative so far, and claims that the drugs must have been planted on him at the race course whilst he was out riding. Not the most original explanation, but he's got no previous form and is sticking to it. He's been charged with possession and up till today has been on remand.'

'And after today?'

'To everyone's astonishment, he's found a couple of people to stand bail for him. Either they're very rich or very silly, because they'll both be one hundred thousand pounds poorer if he flees the country.'

'Do you know who they are?'

'I didn't think to ask. The application's being made this morning before the magistrates and if you like I could give his solicitor a ring this afternoon and find out. On the other hand, it'll be in the racing papers tomorrow for certain.'

'Would you mind? Do you think there's any chance of me talking to James? He rode for me now and again and he at least could clear my mind about Ramirez.'

'There's no law against it, but I can't see him telling you something which he's trying to keep quiet. For all he knows, you could go off and repeat it to the police.'

'I wouldn't dream of it.'

'How can you be so sure? What if he says he's never met Ramirez except on a horse? You'd want to tell the French police that, wouldn't you?'

Alistair nodded sheepishly. 'Anyway, couldn't you at least ask his solicitor if his client is prepared to talk to me?'.

'If you insist. The sergeant gave me his name. It's not a firm I know. I'll give him a call later and ask. Now what else is there to do?'

'My bank manager.'

'Right. If you give me his number, I'll get Sheila to get him and you can speak to him.'

Even though they had moved to New York, Alistair had kept his account with the bank outside Newmarket which he had used as a trainer. It was the same bank who had originally paid for the fateful purchase at Keeneland and they had shown remarkable patience in waiting for him to repay the $1,000,000 and of course the interest on it. The old manager had recently retired, and his successor, the optimistically named Mr Braine, was polite but reticent. He confirmed that an official request had been received for disclosure of any accounts held by Alistair Rye and that he had indeed written to him in New York asking for directions. Was he to disclose details of both accounts?

'What do you mean, both accounts?'

'The current account of course, and the deposit account opened earlier in the year.'

'What deposit account? I've never been in credit, let alone had enough money for a deposit account.'

'I'm sorry, Mr Rye, but according to our records you opened this account in March and at the moment it is showing a substantial balance.'

'There must be a mistake. Are you there this afternoon?'

'Yes, but . . .'

'I'm coming down to see you and I'll be bringing my solicitor.'

Amy looked at him in astonishment. 'Mr Rye, I'm sorry, but I have appointments this afternoon.'

Alistair ignored her protests and kept on talking. 'Yes, that's right, this afternoon. Please can you have all the details waiting?' He put down the receiver and shrugged his shoulders.

'I'm sorry, but this is urgent. He claims I have a deposit account which is rolling in money.'

'And you haven't?'

'It's the first I've ever heard of it.'

'Your wife, possibly?'

'You don't know my wife. She spends money like it's contaminated. It can only be a mistake.'

'I hope so, but in my experience banks don't make errors in their customers' favour except in Monopoly.'

'Will you come?'

'I'll have to look at my diary. I can see you're going to be a very demanding client, Mr Rye.'

'Please call me Alistair.'

'Okay. And you can call me Miss Frost.'

Four hours later they were sitting opposite an ashen-faced bank manager.

'As you see here, Mr Rye, the account was opened by telephone at the beginning of March and in accordance with your instructions statements have been sent care of a post box number in New York.'

'But I never gave any such instructions. Have you asked the assistant who took them over the phone?'

'Miss Davies. I've spoken to her and all she can remember is that it was done by phone and that she wasn't surprised that you wanted the statements sent to America.'

'But what about the bank? Weren't you curious where all this money was coming from? You always were when it was going out of my account.'

'I have to admit that we were a little surprised, but you must remember that you have paid over

£30,000 into your current account over the last six months. Another £50,000 into your deposit account didn't therefore strike us as altogether strange.'

'Where are the payments from?' asked Amy.

'They're all bank transfers from an account in Switzerland.'

'Can you tell us the name?'

'I'm afraid I would need the permission of Head Office.'

'What? Head Office?' Alistair was beginning to lose his patience. 'You have to ask Head Office before you can tell me the source of monies in my own bank account? This is crazy.'

The manager made a pathetic attempt at a smile. 'I don't make the rules, sir.'

'What are you going to tell the police?'

'Unless they produce a court order, I will only tell them exactly what you permit me. You see, at the moment we regard it as a confidential matter between the bank and our client.'

'It all sounds marvellous. Amy, er, Miss Frost, what do you advise?'

'We're going to have to find out where that money came from. Since you've nothing to hide, I think you should show the police everything and leave it to them to trace this Swiss account.'

'But what if it turns up something nasty?'

'How could it?'

'With my luck it's no longer a possibility but a certainty. Okay, Mr Braine, give it all to the police. The only time I'm in credit and I don't want the stuff!'

Alistair and Amy returned to his hotel in Newmarket for tea. The solicitor tried to find out who had stood bail for Eddie James and whether the jockey would now be prepared to talk to him. Alistair was flicking through the catalogue for that evening's sales when she returned from making her call.

'I got through to his lawyer. He was very noncommittal and said he would contact his client and give him your number here. I said you were leaving for America on Monday.'

'Did he say who put up the money?'

'Hold on, I wrote their names down on the back of my chequebook. Neville Harvey was one of them. Do you know him?'

'Yes, he's a trainer who used to put James up on his horses. And the other?'

'Max Stride or Stroud, something like that. Does it ring a bell?'

'Max Stride! I know him all too well. He was responsible for me giving up training. But why would he want to stand bail for Eddie James?'

'I can't help you there; maybe he used to ride for him?'

'Now and again, but not regularly. Why on earth would he do that?'

'Perhaps he thought that James might be safer outside prison than in it.'

'In which case it may be that James knows something after all. I've got to see him. If he doesn't call by tomorrow night I'll have to try and find him myself.'

'That's up to you, but don't expect me to help you. I want to go on practising as a solicitor.'

'Don't worry, I won't do anything to embarrass your professional position. The sales are on to-night; why don't you come along and watch the bidding and have dinner with us afterwards?'

'What would your wife say?'

'Don't worry. I'll phone her in New York and tell her. We'll order a car to drive you back to London afterwards. How does that appeal?'

She hesitated for a moment, but Alistair sensed that she really quite liked the idea.

'Go on, say yes. You can meet my friend Jack Donnelly and he'll keep you amused all evening.'

'But I've got nothing to change into.'

'You look marvellous. If anybody asks you, just say you're my younger sister.'

'And what will you say?'

'That I regard it as a confidential matter between myself and my solicitor.' She laughed, and
Alistair noticed how her whole face lit up. There
was no doubt that Miss Frost was the one bit of
good news in this whole business so far.

Before leaving for the sales, Alistair went to his
room and telephoned Claudia. As it was only
midday in New York he was not surprised to find
her out, and he made do with leaving a short
message on the answerphone. He then called
Morrow and told him everything that had happened except for the incident with Hassan. Rightly
or wrongly, he had again decided not to involve
Morrow. Hassan's assault was a score he very
much wanted to settle on his own, without any
help or words of wisdom from his employer. The
good news was that Morrow had decided to fly over
to England to see his expensive purchase and was
planning to arrive the next day and come down to
Newmarket in the evening. Alistair suddenly felt
more relaxed. Morrow's confidence and command
in any given situation acted as a strong boost to his
own morale, and he particularly wanted his employer's guidance on how to deal with Eddie
James. Morrow had agreed that he should try and
see the jockey, but Alistair recognised that ultimately it might well be that the American with

his financial muscle would obtain information more readily than a penniless racing manager.

He had no sooner put the phone down to New York than it rang again.

'Mr Rye? Eddie James.'

'Eddie. You got my message. I'm sorry about all this trouble you're in.'

'Leave it out, Mr Rye. Ramirez told me everything. Thanks a lot for helping me when I was inside.'

'I don't understand what you're talking about. What did Ramirez say about me?'

'Nothing which isn't going to cost you a lot of money unless you want to go down with me.'

'What the hell do you mean by that?'

'I've got no time for games. You can see me tomorrow at my flat, 148 Putney Court, off the top of Putney High Street, at 4 o'clock, and we can discuss it then – and please, Mr Rye, no more of this Mr Innocent business.'

Amy clearly enjoyed that evening's sale; Jack Donnelly kept up a running commentary throughout the bidding and to cap it all they were able to buy the two horses they wanted way below their agreed limit. Even Hassan made his contribution to the fun by not appearing, and with alcohol dulling the pain in Alistair's finger the threesome

134

went off to dinner together in high spirits. Amy could not have been more removed from Alistair's idea of a lawyer. She had read French and Italian at University and when she realised that all that equipped her for was interpreting or understanding menus without asking the waiter, she had decided to take her solicitor's exams. Having qualified she had joined the old firm of Arthurs because her father knew the senior partner who professed never to have read a case in his life and insisted every year on taking time off for Cheltenham, Ascot and Goodwood. He had no objection to Amy applying the same philosophy to her own work, provided she remembered to put her clients' interests first. During dinner, Jack's jokes became bawdier and bawdier but she was always the first to break into unrestrained laughter. To begin with, Alistair had been slightly anxious that she might take offence, but it soon became clear that she was a fun-loving uninhibited girl who had no difficulty in just being her own unpretentious self. For a brief moment he thought that his admiration for her implied some kind of criticism for Claudia, but he told himself that was ridiculous. They were just two very different kinds of women, and were to be appreciated as such.

It was well past two o'clock when they had downed

their last bottle of champagne and a waiter was hoovering around them.

'Amy.' Alistair had been allowed to drop the more formal address after tea. 'It's too late to go back to London. I've got an idea.'

'You dirty beast!' shouted Jack. 'Amy, ignore him, he's drunk. I've got a better idea.'

'Shut up, Jack. That idea of yours has got you into enough trouble already. No, what I think is that you should have my room tonight and I'll sleep on the sofa in Jack's. That all right by you, Jack?'

'I suppose so. I can think of a better arrangement.'

'And you, Amy?'

She hesitated for a moment. 'But I've no clean clothes for tomorrow.'

'No problem. We'll send out for some in the morning.'

'All right then, but don't anybody try waking me until late! Saturday is the day I lie in.'

'It's a promise,' they replied in unison, saluting.

Alistair knocked again on the door but still there was no reply. He was almost hoarse with calling out her name. The earlier anxiety he had felt when his phone call to her room had gone unanswered was now turning to panic. Perhaps something ghastly had happened to her. For all he knew, Hassan had decided to play another dirty trick on him, only it was Amy who had become the unwitting victim. He cursed himself for involving her in this whole business. He was calling out her name and rattling the door handle when he felt a prod in his back.

'Stick 'em up! This is a hold up!'

He had never been so pleased to hear someone's voice. 'Christ, you had me worried. Where've you been?'

'I got up early after all and went into town to buy some clothes. If you'll allow me into my bedroom I can now have a bath and change.'

'I'm sorry. I was just . . .'

'Alistair, are you all right? You look terribly pale. I suppose all that drink last night has got to you.'

'No, it's nothing. I'm fine. When you're dressed, come on down and have a spot of brunch and then if you want I can drive you to London.'

'Don't worry, I'm happy to take a train.'

'No, it's no problem. I've got to go up anyway.'

'Great. I won't ask you why in case you're doing something you shouldn't be.'

Alistair just grinned. He wanted to tell her he was seeing Eddie James, to involve her in his problems, but he knew it was unfair to ask her to do something which might be professionally improper. What was more, he was keeping it from Claudia, too.

He went downstairs to the bar to be greeted by the sight of Jack Donnelly wrestling with a recalcitrant champagne cork, a hapless waiter looking anxiously on.

'Come over here, Alistair and give us a hand. The hair of this dog is proving damn elusive.'

Chapter 12

They were half way to London when Amy announced out of the blue that she was coming with him to see Eddie James.

'Who said I was going to see him?' asked Alistair, pretending not to be taken by surprise.

'It's pretty obvious, isn't it? Just look at the nervous state you're in. You were jumping around like a kitten outside my bedroom this morning, and you looked extremely nervous when you came downstairs last night after making your phone call. It didn't need a great deal of intelligence to put two and two together and work out why you had this sudden urge to go to Town. The way you veered to the right just now confirmed it; you nearly hit a car in the fast lane.'

'There's not much point in pretending, then?'

She shook her head. 'I ought to let you go on your

own, but as my client I feel I have a duty to protect you.'

'I doubt if James will talk with you present.'

'Then I'll wait outside. What time are we due there?'

'Four o'clock at his flat in Putney.'

'Did he say anything on the phone?'

'That's what was so strange. He said Ramirez had told him everything. He sounded, well, almost threatening, as if I had let him down.'

She turned up the music on the radio and stared at the road ahead, saying nothing.

'What do you think?' asked Alistair at last.

'I think you're in big trouble. Our friend Mr James is either under the genuine impression you are tied up with this drugs business or is setting you up. Either way, you are heading for a juicy demand for money.'

'You mean blackmail?'

'I do indeed. It's more important than ever that you have a witness when you see him.'

'Are you sure about this? I mean, you coming along? For all we know, it could turn nasty and that's plainly not part of your duties as my solicitor.'

'Stop playing the hero and for God's sake look where you're driving.'

* * *

James's flat was on the top floor of a mansion block, not far from East Putney underground. As the front door to the block was open, they didn't bother to ring on the entry phone but went straight on up. The common parts had recently been redecorated judging by the smell of emulsion paint in the air. Alistair was struck by how quiet it seemed, more like the country than his idea of London. Amy rang the bell but there was no answer.

'Are you sure he said four?'

'Positive. Try again.' She did, this time pressing continuously for about thirty seconds.

'Shall I try the people in the flat opposite?' asked Alistair.

'Hold on a sec. Let me look through the letter box.'

She knelt down on the concrete floor to look through the brass flap and as she lent against the door it opened.

'That's funny. Perhaps he's gone out and left you a message.'

'Do you think we ought to go in? We could always come back in half an hour.'

'I thought you were the one who was so keen to see him. Come on, let's go and have a look at Mr James's living quarters.'

The front door opened on to a long, narrow hall which ran both to the right and left of them.

'Is anyone here?' shouted Alistair. 'Eddie, it's Alistair Rye.'

There was no sound.

'Come on,' said Amy. 'Let's try this door.' She opened the one almost immediately in front of them and found herself in the sitting room. On the mantelpiece stood photographs of Eddie receiving numerous decanters and cups, and the walls were covered with blown-up prints of him riding winners. Two large white sofas sat facing each other in front of one of those gas fires which look like coal; overall the room looked clean but somewhat impersonal. On a side table lay a half-open copy of that day's *Sporting Life*.

'I think we ought to go,' whispered Alistair. 'He's obviously not here and there's no message.'

Amy either didn't hear or chose to ignore him. She walked over and picked up one of the photographs from the mantelpiece. 'I presume the one in the yellow silks is Eddie, but who are the other two people with him?'

'The tall good-looking one is Max Stride and the other is . . . Let me look at that will you?' Alistair took the frame from her hands. 'Oh yes, this must have been taken at Haydock, a good three years ago.'

'Alistair, who is that?'

'That's my wife Claudia. Don't worry. That was the only time Eddie rode a winner for me. It was on one of Stride's horses, and Claudia was on duty for me as I had runners at another meeting.'

He put the photograph back in its place. 'I think we'd better go now.'

'Not quite yet. Don't you think it's strange that nobody's here and the door's left open?'

'Perhaps he went out in a hurry. You know how it is sometimes.'

'Listen.' She grabbed his arm. 'Did you hear that?'

'Hear what?'

'I distinctly heard the sound of someone moving around. Yes, there it is again.'

A voice inside Alistair shouted out for him to say she was mistaken but he had also heard the sound.

'Where do you think it came from?' he asked softly.

'Next door. Come on, let's go and find out.'

They tiptoed out of the sitting room and turned right down the corridor. This time they heard a light thud from the first room they came to. Alistair knocked on the door and in a rather pathetic voice asked, 'Are you there, Eddie?'

There was no reply, only another thud.

143

'Stop being so wet,' said Amy, throwing open the door. Alistair caught the cat as it leapt in terror towards them. Apart from the initial shock he had never felt so relieved in his life.

Amy just stood beside him roaring with laughter. 'You should've seen your face, Alistair. Come on, we might as well look in the other rooms now.'

Alistair felt much more relaxed, and holding the cat under his arm with one hand, he opened the door of the room at the end of the corridor with a flourish, bowing to Amy as he did so. 'Mademoiselle, your room is ready.'

Her scream shattered the rural tranquillity of Putney Court. Lying across the bed, wearing only his pyjama bottoms, was the lifeless figure of a man, his eyes wide open, staring inanely but blindly at the ceiling above him. Sticking into a protruding vein in Eddie James's arm was a hypo-dermic needle.

'Christ!' said Alistair. 'He's taken an overdose.'

He was moving instinctively towards the body when Amy hauled him back.

'Hold on a moment. Remember what happened the last time you touched what was later identified as the murder weapon?'

'Murder? You're not suggesting that . . . ?'

'I'm not suggesting anything. It could be an accident or suicide for all I know, but we'll leave all

144

that to the police. The first thing we're going to do is dial 999 and get an ambulance here, and the police. Now aren't you glad I came along?'

'Poor Eddie. You're sure he's dead? I mean, it could be that he's just unconscious.'

Amy shook her head. 'Just look at him, his eyes. I've had one or two clients who have ODed. I'm afraid our Eddie's ridden his last winner.'

They returned to the sitting room and made the necessary calls. Two hours later, the body removed and their statements taken, they were allowed to go home.

As they walked to the car, Alistair offered to take Amy back to her flat.

'If you don't mind, I'd rather walk. It's only twenty minutes or so over the bridge and I could do with a bit of fresh air after all this. What are you going to do?'

Alistair looked at his watch. 'Damn. Morrow is coming down to Newmarket tonight and he won't be best pleased if I'm not there to greet him. He'll be even more annoyed at me getting involved with this business. It's bound to be all over the papers. I'd better cut along.'

'Drive carefully. You were bad enough on the way here.'

'When shall I talk to you? To be honest, I've no idea what the hell we're going to do next.'

145

'When do you go back to the States?'

'Officially Tuesday, but I can postpone it for a day if you want.'

'Good. On Monday we can find out the results of the pathology report on James and if you don't mind, I think we ought to start making some inquiries about your friends Hassan and Stride.'

'And how do you propose to do that?'

'I'll start with my friends at the Yard. The first thing to find out is whether they have a record, and secondly where their money comes from. Sometimes the one explains the other.'

'And the third thing?'

'How about what they were doing the evening Ramirez was murdered?'

'But I saw them both at the casino.'

'And they saw you. How marvellous! You can provide each other with an alibi. Alistair, you've got to start realising the danger you're in before you end up under a guillotine.'

'What? They don't still have that in France, do they?'

'They have, but no-one's had their head cut off since goodness knows when. You never know, they might revive it for a latter-day Sydney Carton who peddled drugs and then murdered one, or possibly two, of his carriers.'

146

'What do you mean, two?'

'Eddie James. You don't think he shut his own cat up in a room like that, do you?'

'Darling, where have you been? I was beginning to get worried.' Alistair wheeled round in astonishment at the sound of Claudia's voice. She was coming down the stairs as he was standing at reception asking for his room key.

'Claudia? What the hell are you doing here? There's nothing wrong, is there?'

She walked over and kissed him on the cheek. 'Aren't you pleased to see me? We were given a weekend off before the dress rehearsal on Tuesday, and Wayne insisted I fly over with him as a surprise for you.'

'And where is the great man himself?'

'In the bar with Jack Donnelly and Etienne, talking about racehorses, what else?'

'Etienne? What's he doing here?'

'Didn't you know? He flew over from France this morning and we all drove down together from London this afternoon. You look surprised.'

'Not really. It's just that when I talked to Wayne yesterday in New York he didn't say anything about Etienne coming over.'

She shrugged her shoulders. 'Don't ask me. On

the way down he and Wayne talked about this
yearling you've just bought, and I rather gathered
that Etienne wants to train him.'

'Did Morrow say he could?'

'I fell asleep on the motorway, so I don't know if
anything was agreed, but before I dozed off I rather
got the impression that Wayne was noncommittal.'

Alistair was glad that no decision had yet been
made. He certainly had nothing against Etienne
personally and no-one could question his ability to
train – Philanderer's success in the Arc proved
that. It was just that at the moment anything
French gave him a sinking feeling in the pit of his
stomach. He had hoped that the horse would stay
in England and be trained by Toby Hartley and
therefore ridden by Willie Grange as his stable
jockey.

They went together to the bar where Morrow,
Lafayette and Donnelly were deep in conversation. They were arguing over the merits of different stallions, and as always Etienne was becoming increasingly excited.

'Calm down, Etienne,' said Alistair, 'and buy
Claudia and me a drink.'

'Ah, Alistair! We were wondering where you
were. Everything go all right in town?' asked
Morrow as he got up from his chair to offer it to

Claudia. 'Your wife was beginning to worry about you.'

Alistair hesitated before replying. He would have preferred not to have mentioned his visit to James, but since it was bound to come out in the papers he decided it was sensible to come clean there and then. 'I'm afraid not. Eddie James is dead.'

'Dead? Eddie James the jockey?' It was Jack Donnelly's turn to sound surprised. 'But when? How?'

'I went to see him this afternoon in the hope that he might be able to help me over this Ramirez business, but when we got to his flat we discovered him dead in his bedroom.'

'Who's we?' asked Claudia.

'Me and Amy Frost; she's a solicitor who's helping me out. It was lucky she was there or I might be facing another murder inquiry.'

'You're not saying he was murdered?'

'At the moment I don't know. We just found him there lying on his bed with a needle sticking out of his arm. Not a very pleasant sight.'

'A drug overdose?'

'That's what the ambulance people said, but at the moment they can't say whether it was suicide, an accident or the work of somebody who wanted Eddie out of the way.'

'And who could that be?' asked Jack Donnelly. 'If a jockey rides a bad race you normally sack him. Murdering him would be a clear breach of the rules of racing.'

'Jack, you're appalling!' said Claudia. 'You can't take anything seriously.'

'Sorry, my darling, but it's the only way I can get through this cruel world of ours. Come on, Alistair, why would anybody want to kill Eddie James?'

'To keep him quiet, perhaps. If James knew too much about a drug-smuggling ring, it could be a very powerful reason for wanting him in an early grave. It could be the same person who disposed of Ramirez.'

'Do you have any ideas?'

'I know who didn't do it, which is more important, and that's me. Anyway that's enough of my problems. What brings you over here, Etienne?'

The French trainer had kept uncharacteristically quiet during the conversation over Eddie James and Alistair couldn't now resist pulling his leg over his sudden interest in the Newmarket sales.

'Nothing really. I just thought that it would be nice, a matter of courtesy to Mr Morrow, if I came and saw what you and Jack had bought for him this week.'

'How touching. Have you seen any of them yet, Wayne?'

150

'Only the fillies. Jack took me over to the stables where they're being looked after for the moment. I'm very pleased with what I saw and we'll have to have a word later over who's going to train them. My present inclination is to send three of them over to you, Etienne, in France and keep three in training here.'

'And the Nijinsky colt?' asked Alistair, teasingly.

'I thought we could go and have a look at him tomorrow. I want to savour the moment I set eyes on the most expensive yearling I've ever purchased.'

'I just hope you're not disappointed. I can tell you that Hassan was, when we outbid him. Isn't that right, Jack?'

The Irishman just smiled. Alistair had told him about the attack but asked him not to mention it to Morrow.

The American went on. 'That'll teach him to threaten me. I don't believe he's got the guts to do anything anyway. Come on, drink up. We're booked into dinner at nine and my stomach thinks my throat's been cut.'

Alistair was subdued throughout dinner and left the talking to Jack and Claudia, who was full of herself and bursting to tell everybody about her 'new play' as she called it. It was to open to the public on the following Wednesday.

'You are going to make the effort to come, Alistair, aren't you?' she asked pointedly. 'When I think of all those dreary racecourses I used to go to . . .'

Alistair could sense the daggers in her eyes even from where he was sitting at the other end of the table. He felt a sudden urge to remind her that she had chosen to marry a racehorse trainer, but thought better of it.

'Of course, darling. I may have to stay on over here for a couple more days, but I intend to fly back that afternoon in time for the show. What about you, Wayne? Are you going to support my wife on her big night?'

'You bet I'll be there, and afterwards I insist on taking you both out to celebrate. I'll book the 21 Club.'

'Wonderful!' shouted Claudia gleefully. She then turned her attention on an unusually quiet Etienne. 'I suppose you'll be flying over too?'

Alistair knew that Claudia supposed no such thing, but she also enjoyed teasing the Frenchman, who devoted a lot of effort to oiling up to his biggest owner.

'I would love to, I really would, but . . .'

'Then it's done!' bellowed Wayne. 'It'll be a good time for you and Alistair to get together to decide next year's plans. You'll have some pretty fancy yearlings to train for me. Don't look so worried; I'll pay your air fare over.'

Etienne immediately cheered up and Alistair sensed that he had taken Morrow's invitation as a sign that he was in line to train the Nijinsky colt.

'Not yet, *mon vieux*,' murmured Alistair to himself. 'Not yet.'

Claudia turned on him as soon as they were in bed.

'You were in bloody good form tonight. I come all this way and you can hardly raise a smile.'

'I'm sorry, but things aren't looking too good over this Ramirez business.'

'What do you mean "not too good"? The police have got my statement and it ties in with yours because you told me what to say.'

'Hang on a minute. I only reminded you what happened. There's a hell of a difference. That French lawyer has been on the phone and says that they still regard me as the number one suspect, and apparently the French police want to come over and interview you personally. They're taking this drug smuggling stuff seriously and trying to put me in the middle of it. That's why I had to go and see Eddie James.'

'I don't follow,' she said sulkily.

'Don't you remember? Or maybe I didn't tell you. He was found with a load of heroin on him after

York races and the police now reckon that he and Ramirez were in it together.'

'Nothing would surprise me about that Mexican. Didn't James ride for us once?'

'You've got a good memory. He rode one of Max Stride's horses at Haydock when you were standing in for me.'

'Where were you, then?'

'At Kempton or somewhere. The horse won anyway, and James had a photograph of you and Stride on his mantelpiece.'

'God, I remember now. I was looking dreadful that day. I had food poisoning or something.'

'You looked all right to me. While we're on the subject of Max Stride, when you spoke to him at the casino that night, you didn't perhaps mention my fight with Ramirez?'

'Of course not. You told me not to tell anybody. He might have made some mention about the cut on your eye but I certainly didn't tell him how you got it. Why?'

'Because it's possible that whoever did murder Ramirez had found out about the fight and has used it to sew me up.'

'That's ridiculous. Why would anybody want to do that? Your trouble is you read too many detective stories.'

'That may be, but truth can be stranger than

fiction. Don't you think it's curious that Eddie James should be found dead the very day I arrange to meet him?'

'Not necessarily. When did he get out of prison?'

'Yesterday.'

'Which could mean that he was desperate for a fix and went over the top. What makes you think it was murder?'

'The look on his face, and the cat.'

'The cat? What cat?'

'It's nothing. Just something Amy said.'

'If you ask me, this Amy sounds like the one who needs a solicitor. Either that or the pair of you should see a psychiatrist. If I didn't know you better I'd think you fancied her. What does she look like?'

'I haven't really noticed. Nothing special.'

'Liar. Go to sleep and try not to have any bad dreams,' she said, rolling over as she did so, to lie with her back to him.

'Good night, Claudia.'

Ten minutes later Alistair was having his first nightmare.

Chapter 13

On Monday morning Alistair waved good-bye to Claudia and Wayne at Heathrow and headed back to London. His boss had duly inspected his latest purchase and pronounced himself satisfied with the yearling's looks and conformation. What was more, he had asked Alistair who he would recommend as trainer and had given the go-ahead when he had suggested Toby Hartley. Alistair knew that Toby would be over the moon to land such a well-bred addition to his yard. It would also undoubtedly make it less easy for him to turn nasty, if and when it came out about Willie Grange passing on information in breach of the rules of racing.

Amy was waiting for him at her offices and the anxious look on her face made it clear that there was bad news.

'Your bank manager's been on the phone. The

police called him into work over the weekend and he handed over the details of your alleged deposit account. From what I gather he was only able to give them the dates and amounts of the payments in, together with copies of the monthly statements they sent to the post box number in New York.'

'Did he tell you who's been paying this money into my account?'

'Only that it's come from a numbered account in a Swiss bank, Banque du Citoyen. Do you know it?'

'Never heard of it. Swiss banks aren't one of my specialities. Don't we know the name of the account holder?'

'Not yet. The Swiss are about as informative as British Rail. Lately they've been prepared to disclose snippets of information but only when there's serious crime involved.'

'What about this case, then?'

'Maybe. We'll soon know, anyway. I took the liberty of talking to the police officer dealing with it this morning and he's coming round to see you here for a friendly chat in . . .' she looked at her watch '. . . about ten minutes.'

'Here? Is that wise?'

'I think it's essential you're seen to cooperate. The police are treating the deaths of Ramirez and James as part of the same inquiry and since you're a suspect in France it's inevitable that you're a central part of their investigations.'

'Is there any news about James?'

'The provisional autopsy report shows that he died from a massive overdose of heroin. Apparently his body showed no sign of previous drug abuse, which, together with the bruising on his arm, suggests that the injection, let alone the dose, was anything but voluntary.'

'You mean, someone held his arm and forcibly injected the drug?'

'It looks that way.'

'And the time of death?'

'They can't be specific. Anything between half an hour to three hours before we arrived.'

'So at least this is one murder which I can't be blamed for.'

'It looks that way. It's just lucky I came with you, otherwise you might well have had some explaining to do.'

'Any news on Stride or Hassan?'

'Give me a chance. It's not just a question of looking up their past in *Timeform*, you know.'

'I'm sorry,' said Alistair. 'If we could just show the police that one or either of them has a criminal record they might just start digging into their backgrounds and discover where all their money's coming from.'

159

'But what's to connect them to all this, apart from your understandable desire for revenge?'

'If what Willie Grange has heard is true, they both had some kind of relationship with Ramirez. The Deauville race, for all we know, could just have been a small part of it.'

'It's possible, I suppose.'

The ringing of the phone interrupted them.

'It looks like the police are here. Whatever you do, don't get angry, and if you don't know how to answer any particular question, then leave it to me.'

Inspector Holdsworth was a straight-talking, no-nonsense Yorkshireman, whose florid cheeks hinted at a partiality to the occasional evening devoted to the consumption of the odd gallon of bitter. His assistant, Detective-Constable Charlton, had the self-confident air of a man who spent his life tipping outsiders to his friends. They made no attempt to make Alistair feel at ease, but launched at once into the offensive.

'Mr Rye, could you tell us when and why you opened this account in Switzerland?' asked the inspector in a caustic tone which no doubt had taken many years to cultivate.

'I know nothing about it, Inspector. I had no idea I even had a deposit account in this country until the bank manager told me on Friday, let alone one in Switzerland.'

'Really? And what about the monthly statements which were sent to you in New York? Go astray, did they?' His tone had now graduated to the sarcastic.

Alistair just managed to resist rising to the bait. 'I never saw any of those statements. I'm told they were sent to a postal box number address in New York. For all I know they're still there now, uncollected and unopened.'

'They're not. We've checked with New York and nothing's there.'

'That doesn't prove anything. Whoever opened the account could just as easily pose as me and collect them.'

'How many people knew you had an account near Newmarket?'

'Loads. All my owners for a start, and anybody to whom I've ever made out a cheque. Have you found out who was making the payments in from Switzerland? The name of my so-called benefactor?'

'We have, as a matter of fact. The Swiss bank has been remarkably cooperative, but then nobody likes drug pushers, do they?'

Alistair chose not to answer. This could hardly be described as a friendly chat.

'Before we deal with that further, I wonder, Mr

Rye, if you could explain about the cash payments into your credit account? £30,000 is a lot of money even for you racing people.'

Alistair looked towards Amy. He had no desire to get Willie Grange into trouble but it was plain that he had to give some sort of explanation.

'I won it gambling.'

'On the horses?' The mocking tone in the inspector's voice said it all.

'On the horses, Inspector. As you can imagine, with my racing background I have access to some pretty good information.'

'Very good, by the sound of it. No doubt you could identify the names of the horses, the races they won and the amount of your winnings?'

'If you insist. I've done all my betting through a commission agent, so he should be able to provide an accurate record.'

'A commission agent?'

'Yes. Someone who puts bets on for a commission, hence the name.'

'His name, please.'

'Do I have to?'

Amy now intervened. 'I think so, Mr Rye.'

'Okay. His name's Rafferty, Fingers Rafferty.'

'And who provided you with this valuable information?'

162

'I'm not prepared to say.'

'Are you sure about that? I can't see why you should want to keep it a big secret.' Alistair noticed the inspector giving his assistant a knowing wink.

'Positive.'

'As you like, Mr Rye. Make a note of that, Charlton, will you? Now, where were we? Oh yes, this account of yours in Switzerland.'

'What do you mean, "of mine"? I told you, I know nothing about it.'

'Very convenient to store the proceeds of drug smuggling in a fictitious name. All the big villains do it.'

'I resent that. Amy, do I have to listen to all this?' Alistair rose as if to leave but she signalled him to calm down.

'Mr Rye, please sit down. The inspector's only doing his job, although I must say I find his tone at times a little unhelpful.'

Inspector Holdsworth smiled at the solicitor but made no attempt to apologise. This was a role he had obviously played a hundred times and there was no question of any change in his lines now.

'Don't worry, Mr Rye, I've only got one more question. As I said a moment ago, we know the name of this account in Switzerland.'

'Well, Inspector?'

'Do you know someone called Jean Gerard?'

Alistair blushed briefly and hesitated before replying. 'No, Inspector, I know no-one of that name.'

'Are you sure? For a moment I thought I detected a sign of recognition in your reaction.'

'No, I'm quite positive I don't.'

'In those circumstances, I've nothing more to ask you, at least for the moment. I understand from the Deauville police that you can expect to see Inspector Renard in the very near future and in the meantime, of course, we will be pursuing our own inquiries. Thank you both for seeing us at such short notice. We'll show ourselves out, Miss Frost.'

They had no sooner left than Amy asked, 'Alistair, are you all right? You looked knocked for six when the inspector asked you about Jean Gerard. You don't know him, do you?'

'I doubt very much whether Jean Gerard exists. By sheer coincidence it just happens to be the name of a horse I once trained, a very fast two-year-old, by Brigadier Gerard. Whoever opened that damned account knows a lot about me.'

'And who owned Jean Gerard?'

'Max Stride, who else?'

For a few moments neither bothered to speak. It was now clear that Alistair was caught in a web which had been spun over a considerable period of time; far from helping him escape from it, the police were intent on making it permanent.

Eventually it was Amy who broke the silence. 'There's no point hanging around here with a long face. How about a spot of lunch and a drink to cheer us up?'

'Good idea. Where shall we go?'

'There's a pub just around the corner if you're happy with a sandwich and don't mind over-hearing the odd lawyer banging on about what he told his Lordship in court this morning.'

'Sounds fine. We can plan what we do next. At the moment I feel that I'm heading for a prolonged stay in a French jail.'

'Don't start getting gloomy, for God's sake. Somewhere out there is the man who murdered Ramirez and also, if the police are right, the mastermind behind a vast drug-smuggling organisation. We've just got to go out and find him.'

'Amy, you make it all sound so easy, like the second half of one of those television programmes where the villains always get caught. Real life strikes me as being a touch different.'

'Come on. "Never weaken" is my family motto.'

They found themselves a table in the corner of the pub and Amy drew up a list of possible suspects.

'Firstly there's Stride. We have to find out what he was doing on the evening of the Deauville race before you saw him in the casino. Any ideas?'

'I'll try Willie Grange. Rough Diamond was ridden that day by an English jockey and it's just possible that they all had a victory dinner together in the evening.'

'Secondly there's Hassan. We know he was at the casino but at the moment have no idea of his movements between the time Ramirez left your villa and when you saw him.'

'Of course, that supposes he himself stabbed the Mexican. Any one of his henchmen could have done it while Hassan tucked into a large dinner at his hotel.'

'It's possible, but his evident glee when your nail was extracted makes me think he enjoys being present at the scene of the crime. Do you know where he was staying?'

'I'm pretty certain he was at the Normandy. I've stayed there a few times myself over the years and I might be able to find out something from one of the receptionists. It's a long shot, though.'

'Outsiders do come in now and again! Then there's Etienne.'

'Etienne? Don't be ridiculous. He's far too precious to hurt a fly. He'd rather die than get blood on one of his hand-made shirts.'

'How can you be so sure? He saw Ramirez regularly and what better base for a drugs warehouse than a respectable training establishment in Chantilly? What's more, he was in London on Saturday, and what's to have stopped him paying a surprise call on Eddie James and silencing him before travelling down to Newmarket?'

Alistair shook his head. 'No, Amy. It sounds plausible, but you just don't know Etienne.'

'All right, so I don't know him, but maybe that's an advantage. I've never acted for a criminal yet whose mother wouldn't swear he couldn't hurt a fly. Do you know what he was doing on the night of Ramirez's murder?'

'No. All I know is that he claims not to have seen him after the races that day.'

'You'd better find out his movements, then. Check with his head lad what time he got back to Chantilly, then make up some pretext for asking Etienne himself what he did that night.'

'Is that it then?'

'No, there's one more. Your boss, Morrow.'

Alistair smiled. 'That's the one person we definitely can rule out. He was in Paris the evening Ramirez was murdered. I even talked to him myself.'

'All right, then, we'll cross him off the list. How's your sandwich?'

'Pretty good. Do you want another drink?'

'Why not? And then you can tell me all about Claudia.'

'Why do you want to hear about her?'

'Because she interests me.'

'On one condition.'

'And what's that?'

'You tell me all about the man in your life.'

She grinned. 'That's easy. He's six feet tall, has big brown eyes, is kind and understanding, has a gentle sense of humour and puts his family and friends before himself.' She paused. 'Oh yes, and he's devastatingly romantic in bed.'

Alistair felt an overwhelming sense of envy of this unknown lover. 'And what's his name?'

'I don't know. I haven't met him yet.'

Alistair breathed a sigh of relief. At least he had brown eyes!

When they returned to her office a large buff envelope was waiting on her desk. Amy opened it and glanced quickly at the two sheets of paper it contained.

'It's from my friend at the Yard,' she explained. 'He says that they've nothing on their computers on anyone called Max Stride, which means that he's either kept to the straight and narrow or more likely, if your character assessment is any good, just never been caught. He's been luckier with

168

Hassan though, and has sent over a résumé of his past.' She held up a sheet of paper upon which Alistair could see a couple of paragraphs of writing. 'Shall I read it out or would you like to read it for yourself?'

'No, go on. I'll sit here and listen.'

She cleared her throat and began. 'Hassan, Ahmed. Also known to use a variety of other names, all of which are unpronounceable, I'm afraid. First arrested in 1961 in Marseilles for running large-scale prostitution racket but acquitted at trial after principal witness found murdered, with both her hands cut off. Convicted 1964 of living off immoral earnings in Nice and sentenced to six months' imprisonment. Suspected by French police of smuggling arms into France and then on to Syria and of controlling prostitution in the whole of South West France. Has large interests in pornography and vice clubs in Soho but so far insufficient evidence has been obtained to warrant an arrest. Extremely dangerous. Known sadist and always accompanied by at least three bodyguards, all thought to be armed and extremely violent. Do not attempt to arrest unless armed.'

'Is that it?' asked Alistair when she stopped reading. 'Nothing about drugs?'

'It's enough, isn't it? Just the sort of chap to make up a foursome at bridge.'

'It's hard to believe that sort of man is allowed to own racehorses.'

'Alistair, the Jockey Club licence trainers, not owners. Perhaps that's where they're going wrong?'

Alistair laughed. 'He's certainly got the right credentials to be our villain. Something inside me, though, still says that Stride's our man.'

'That's wish being mother to the thought. Tomorrow we'll start making some inquiries about him, but you can begin now by telling me where he lives and whether he has any companies we can check out.'

'He's a flat in Eaton Square and as for companies, I don't remember him ever telling me about his business interests. Hold on a moment; I remember once he gave me a cheque and I was rather surprised that it was not drawn on his own personal account. What was the name? I remember thinking it was familiar. I've got it. M and S International, it was called. I remember making some joke about not knowing he owned Marks and Spencers.'

'That's a start. I'll get a company search done straight away. If there is such a company registered, it will also tell us about any other directorships he may have. Why don't you contact Willie and get him working on Rough Diamond's jockey.'

'He's riding today at Lingfield and won't be back until late this evening.'

'What time's the last race?'

'4.30. Good idea. If I leave now I can catch him on the course. Can I call you later?'

'I'll phone you. Where are you staying?'

'At the Berkeley in Knightsbridge. If you feel peckish I'd love to buy you dinner.'

'Thanks, but I've a lot of work to clear up here. Good luck with Willie.'

He ran down the stairs and hailed a cab which had just dropped a group of prosperous-looking individuals, on their way no doubt to take advice from some very expensive Queen's Counsel. The cabby looked surprised to be asked to go to Lingfield races but cheered up immediately when Alistair offered him an extra ten pounds if he got there by 4.15. As for his fare, all he could think of on the journey was his ever-increasing infatuation for his lawyer.

Chapter 14

By the time Alistair reached Lingfield Park race-course the runners were cantering down to the start for the sixth and final race of the day. It was for maiden two-year-olds and had attracted a large field of twenty-four runners. Willie was riding a chestnut filly which had come sixth in her first, and to date only, run this season and he had mentioned to Alistair on Sunday night that the horse was hotly fancied and the stable was going, in his words, for a 'right touch'. Alistair was a gambler at heart and he had no intention of allowing his immediate problems to distract him from having a little wager. He told himself that if the horse won it would be a sure sign that his luck was now in and that the present nightmare would soon be over. By the time he reached his usual bookmaker on the rails the horses were about to come under starter's orders and Princess Caroline, as the certainty was called, had come down from 5 to 1 to 7 to 2 joint favourite. In racing there is no such thing as a well-kept secret and this gamble was plainly no exception. Alistair called a bet of seven hundred to two hundred pounds and rushed up into the stands to watch the race. Since he didn't have his binoculars with him and the runners were coming straight down the six-furlong course towards him, he had little chance of picking up the colours in the early stages but it was clear from the racecourse commentary that Princess Caroline was going nicely in about fifth position just off the rails on the stand side. Entering the final furlong there were still at least six horses in with a chance, although Princess Caroline had now taken up the lead and held about half a length advantage. For a cold autumnal day there was a surprisingly large crowd and judging by the roar that now went up each and every one of them had been let into the stable's confidence. Alistair joined in the encouragement eagerly. He was just counting his winnings when the filly started to weaken and at her quarters appeared a fast-finishing grey being driven as if the jockey's life, and that of his children as well, depended on it. With fifty yards to go the horses matched strides, but then to Alistair's dismay the grey began to draw away and to a deafening silence passed the post a good half length to the good. That was bad enough, but to add to his misery Alistair knew that the winning colours were familiar. He turned round and asked a man standing behind him if he could look at his race card and his worst fears were confirmed – Ahmed Hassan was the lucky owner.

There was at least one consolation. Rough Diamond's jockey, Vic Scott, had also been riding in the race and Willie had agreed to bring him with him to the bar after they had weighed in.

Although Scott had never ridden for Alistair they were on nodding acquaintance terms and it only needed a couple of glasses of champagne to loosen his tongue. He told Alistair that there had indeed been a party at Deauville on the evening of Rough Diamond's victory.

'What time did it start?' asked Alistair. 'And where was it held?'

'We had it in Mr Stride's suite at the Royal Hotel. Bloody nice it was too. It got underway at about nine o'clock and finished in the early hours of the morning.'

'And was Mr Stride there when you arrived?'

Scott hesitated for a moment. He wasn't regarded

as one of the more intelligent of flat-racing jockeys and the act of casting his mind back caused him to look tortured.

'No, come to think of it he wasn't. He arrived about half an hour later.'

'You wouldn't know why, by any chance?'

'No idea, I just ride his horses, but I remember somebody saying as a joke that he had gone to pay off Ramirez. Is. there any more in that bottle, guv'nor?'

Alistair helped Scott and Willie to another glass. He didn't want to appear too inquisitive and he also doubted whether the jockey had any more information to give. He decided to change the subject.

'What about Eddie James then? Terrible business, that.'

Scott nodded. 'I read in the *Life* this morning that you discovered the body, Mr Rye. Horrible for you. Who could imagine him killing himself like that? I suppose there must have been something in this drug business after all.'

Alistair played the innocent. 'Surely not? It must have been planted on him, all that heroin.'

'That's not what they're saying in the jockeys' room. The word is that James and Ramirez were in it together and that some big name in racing is behind them.'

Alistair looked anxiously at Willie. 'Have they mentioned any names, Vic?'

For some reason the jockey pretended not to hear and instead downed the remaining champagne in his glass.

'Sorry, must go or I'll miss my lift back to Lambourn. Nice seeing you again, Mr Rye, and I was sorry about Ramirez.'

'Why do you think he suddenly clammed up?' Alistair asked Willie as soon as Scott was out of earshot.

The jockey shook his head. 'No idea. Unless, of course, you're the big name being mentioned and he felt embarrassed.'

'But wouldn't you have heard the rumour?'

'It's not likely. Remember, everyone knows I'm a friend of yours, so they probably do their whispering when I'm out of the room.'

'But why would he want to be seen with me if I was considered such bad news?'

'To be honest, Alistair, he wasn't very keen to come and have a drink in the first place. I had to persuade him that it would only take a few minutes and there was nothing to worry about. His attitude's no different from the rest of them. He doesn't want to know where the owner's money comes from. After all he's a jockey, not a tax inspector.'

'From what he told us, Stride could have gone to meet Ramirez and murdered him in time to return to the party.'

'But how about the body? How did it get from Honfleur to where it was found?'

'I suppose in the boot of a car, in the early hours of the morning. One of the advantages of Ramirez's villa, from a murderer's point of view that is, was that it was set back from the road and you had to go up a short dirt track to get there. In other words, nicely hidden from the public gaze.'

'Very convenient. Where do we go from here? Is there anything I can do?'

'Hassan's next on our list. Amy Frost has discovered that he's big in prostitution and pornography, and no doubt one or two of his former business associates are propping up a flyover in France. If I can find out the names of his minders, is there any chance of the lads making a few discreet inquiries for me?'

'Are you suggesting what I think you're suggesting?'

'I don't want them hurt or anything. Just persuaded to give a little information about their master's movements on the night of that race.'

Alistair looked at the bandage on the index finger of his right hand. Settling his score with Hassan would clearly have to wait for the time being.

* * *

There were no messages waiting for him when he arrived back at his hotel. He had hoped that Amy might have called, and he felt annoyed with himself for wanting so much to hear from her. He now accepted that his interest was not purely professional, yet he kept on telling himself that Claudia had always been loyal to him and that now if ever he had to remain loyal to her. The trouble was that such sentiments were more easily conceived than executed. Returning to his room, he telephoned New York to see if Claudia had got back safely. Part of him hoped that she wouldn't answer, as he was certain that something in his voice or manner would give him away – the psychological manifestation of guilt. He let the number ring for thirty seconds and put the phone down. After lying on the bed for ten minutes he decided there was no point in staring at the ceiling and hoping that Amy would call; he might as well have a bath, shave and go and have dinner on his own in the hotel restaurant.

Half an hour later he was sitting in the bar sipping a martini. A quick analysis of his present position scarcely cheered him up; it would only be a matter of time before the police found out that Jean Gerard was the name of one of his horses and it did not take too much of an intellectual leap to suggest that he had opened the bank account in Switzerland. Of course the police had no way of proving that he had, but for that matter nor could he prove that he hadn't. Whoever was behind this drug ring had certainly laid his escape route well – with all roads leading to Rye.

He looked round the bar where the head waiter was taking orders from prospective diners. In the corner, sitting on his own, he noticed a middle-aged man reading, or more accurately hiding behind, a copy of the *Daily Telegraph*. Dressed in a grey suit, he looked out of place and uncomfortable in the luxurious surroundings of the hotel. Alistair was certain that he had seen him somewhere before, but he just couldn't put a name or even a place to the face. He ordered another martini. At the moment he felt wary of everybody and everything and he constantly expected the clink of Inspector Renard's hand-cuffs and the recital of the French version of the caution.

He treated himself to a bottle of extremely fine claret during dinner and it was only as he lingered over coffee and ran through the race at Lingfield in his mind that it came to him where he had seen the man in the bar before – he had been the owner of the race card he had borrowed. The police must be suspicious if they were now having him followed.

Not surprisingly he couldn't sleep. He kept on seeing Stride's face grinning at him from the other side of prison bars and whenever he did manage to doze off, he dreamt of Claudia taunting him for having fallen for Amy. It was a relief when morning came, and his spirits were lifted even further by the unexpected arrival of Amy to have breakfast with him. She had brought with her the preliminary results of the company searches into Stride's activities and was bursting to tell him her news.

'I really think we might be on to something. M and S does exist and Stride is given as one of the directors. The company hasn't filed any accounts for two years and those for two years ago show that it was running at a substantial loss.'

'What's its line of business?'

'It says import export, which as you know can cover a multitude of sins. What's more interesting is that it apparently has offices in France and New York. Do you see what I'm getting at?'

Alistair nodded, pretending to understand. 'Go on.'

'If you wanted to transport drugs from America to France, what better cover than a legitimate business front? Obviously your friend was making money somehow, because he couldn't afford a string of sausages, let alone racehorses, on the profits of the business as disclosed in these accounts.'

'Did you find out if he has any other directorships?'

'Yes, one other, a property company called Stride International Limited. That hasn't filed any accounts for five years and according to the last set it's also running at a loss.'

'Where are the offices?'

'The accounts only have to give the registered address. Fortunately it's the same as M and S Limited, so I suggest you finish that cup of coffee and we can go round and have a look for ourselves. It's just north of Oxford Street. If we get a cab we could be there to greet the workers as they arrive, if there are any.'

The registered offices of Stride International and M and S Limited consisted of a single room on the third floor of a dingy office building off Baker Street. The door was locked and the pile of mail which could be spotted lying on the floor through the letter box suggested that neither company was actively trading. Eventually Alistair and Amy located the caretaker whose initial hostility soon turned to garrulousness after her palm was crossed with a ten-pound note.

'Funny kind of businesses, if you ask me. No-one ever works there, you know, but once a month, sometimes twice, this gentleman comes and picks up the mail.'

'Can you describe him?' asked Alistair.

'Taller than you, about six foot I'd say, and very good-looking I suppose, if you like that sort. Rude bugger, though, never so much as a hello or a tip at Christmas.'

'And his mail? Have you ever noticed where that comes from?' inquired Amy.

'Can't say I have. With all these offices to look after I don't have enough time to study every letter, you know.'

'Just think for a moment. Did he ever get packages from abroad, from France or America perhaps?'

The caretaker shook her head. 'Not that I can remember. He did get the odd parcel from Amsterdam though, always marked "Fragile". I remember that because my grandson wanted the stamps and when I asked the gentleman if I could have them he told me to mind my own business. Bloody charming, if you ask me.'

They said goodbye and took a cab to Amy's offices. They were no nearer finding out how Stride earned his living and Alistair was wondering what they could do next.

'Amsterdam. Isn't that one of the drug centres of Europe?' he asked Amy.

'No more so than, say, London or Marseilles. It's diamonds you're thinking of.'

Alistair was silent for a couple of minutes. Then, 'You said this morning that Stride was one of the directors of M and S. Does that mean there are others?'

Amy opened her briefcase and took out the documents which had been obtained from the Registrar of Companies.

'Quite honestly I don't remember, I was just pleased to see his name. Hold on while I have a look.' She rustled through the papers until she found the document she wanted. 'Here it is. Notice of change of directors. On June 20, 1985, a C. Tucker became a director. There's no indication of sex and the address given is the same as Stride's in Eaton Square.'

'Did you say C. Tucker?' Alistair sounded agitated.

Amy nodded. 'That's right. Does it ring a bell?'

'I hope not. You see, Tucker was Claudia's maiden name. You don't think that . . . ?' He chose not to finish the question.

Amy's first task on arriving at her office was to phone her contact at Scotland Yard and find out the names of Hassan's bodyguards. Fortunately the sole qualification for that position was a disposition to gratuitous violence and with that came every chance of a criminal record. Twenty minutes later her call was returned and with it, 'off the record', came the names of two known associates of the Moroccan. One was Algerian and the other French but fortunately the latter had a last-known address in South London. It was a slim hope that he might be found there, but Alistair had reached the stage when any lead, however slender, was worth following up.

Amy wrote out the address and handed it to him.

'Are you going to see him yourself? Because if you are, I'm coming with you.'

He couldn't help but admire her enthusiasm and courage.

'I'm not. Wherever I go at the moment trouble seems either to be expecting me or following in my footsteps. Anyway, I wouldn't have much chance with an eighteen-stone heavy; I hardly reckon he'd respond to reasoned argument or a plea to help a chap in trouble.'

'Absolutely right. What are you going to do, then?'

'Willie has some "friends" who are going to pop round and ask a few pertinent questions.'

'They won't be violent, will they?' For the first time there was a trace of anxiety in her voice. 'You see, that information in your hand is confidential to the police. It shouldn't have been given to me in the first place. If anything hapens to this man I'll be for the high jump.'

'Don't worry. Willie's lads won't harm a hair on his head, although I can't say they might not frighten him a little.'

'Don't let me down on this, will you? Promise?'

'I promise. What's next on the agenda?'

'I'm going to keep on making inquiries about Stride. I thought I'd find out if the boys at Customs and Excise have anything on him. It's a long shot, but you never know. And you, what about going over to France and trying to find out about Etienne's movements on the night of the murder? You could fly over this afternoon and go from there to New York.'

'Oh.' Alistair sounded taken aback. 'I was hoping that you might have dinner with me.'

'Dinner? Alistair, you just don't seem to realise the need for urgency at the moment. You could literally be arrested and charged any day now. Probably the only thing that's holding them back is establishing a direct link between you and the drugs. And they're probably working on that

now, both over here and in France, and for all
we know, on the other side of the Atlantic as
well. Go on, fly to Paris this afternoon and drive
down to Chantilly. If Etienne's there, you can
always make some excuse about popping in to
see the horses.'

'In fact he's probably left already for New York
for the first night of Claudia's play.'

'Good. Then you'd better get cracking.'

'All right, but under the terms of my release from
custody I'm obliged to tell the French police if I
enter France. Do you think I should?'

'Why not? If they somehow found out you were
there and you hadn't told them, all hell would
break loose. I'll telephone that chap Renard for
you at Deauville and say you'll be staying at –
where is it?'

'La Tremoille.'

'La Tremoille in Paris on your way back to New
York.'

'Thanks, you're a wonder.'

'You can tell that to my senior partner when this
is all over,' Amy laughed.

Early next morning Alistair drove down to Chantilly from Paris in a hired car. The last time he had
made the trip was the Friday before the Arc and he

found it hard to believe that is life could have
changed so dramatically in such a short time.
Although the flat season in France was drawing to a
close there was still the usual buzz of activity
around the yard, and Henri, Etienne's head lad,
was in the middle of things, barking commands to
the stable lads and girls as they prepared the horses
for their morning exercise. He was surprised to see
Alistair arrive, and did not go out of his way to be
that friendly.

'Monsieur Lafayette has gone to America. He
won't be back before the weekend.'

'I know. I spent last night in Paris and thought I'd
just pop down to see Philanderer before flying back
to New York this morning.'

'If you had said you were coming, I'd have
kept him back for second lot. He's already on the
gallops.'

'Ah well, never mind. Any news about Ramirez?'

Henri gave him a questioning look, as if to say
'You know more about that than I do'. 'The police
were down here the other day asking questions
about him, and poking their noses into our business. They wanted to know how often we had
runners in England and what kind of kit he used to
take with him.'

'Was that all?'

'It's enough, isn't it? I gathered they'd just searched his apartment.'

'Did they find anything?' asked Alistair, a shade too eagerly.

'I'm not in their confidence, but I did see a whole lot of his riding kit on the back seat of their car. They forgot to take the stuff he had left here, though.'

'What stuff?'

'A couple of helmets and a whip.'

'Where are they now?'

'Where they left them, in the tack room. Unless there's anything else?' Henri made as if to move off.

Alistair wasn't certain how to raise the next topic. 'Just one thing, Henri. You couldn't tell me what time Monsieur Lafayette got back the evening of the Deauville race?'

The head lad made no reply and Alistair continued awkwardly: 'It's just that I telephoned him that night and I'm trying to pinpoint the time of that call.' It was a clumsy lie and he knew that Henri saw it as such.

'He returned about ten thirty. I know because Philanderer arrived back in his box about half an hour before and I was still supervising things in the yard. Now, if you'll excuse me? If I were you, I would go back to Paris,' he concluded meaningfully.

Henri turned and went off to one of the boxes in the far corner of the yard. Alistair knew that he had gone red with embarrassment and rather than drive away immediately, he decided to ignore Henri's suggestion and relax by wandering about the yard and looking at one or two of the horses. Five minutes later he found himself by the tack room and he could not resist going in to have a quick look at the remains of Ramirez's kit. Thrown in the corner he could see two helmets and a twelve-inch whip. He picked up one of the helmets and for some reason tried it on, remembering the days when he himself used to ride out as a trainer. The helmet seemed unusually heavy and narrow; he could hardly fit it over his head. Taking it off he felt inside. Instead of being flat the lining was soft and bulging. He laid it on a nearby table and taking a pen-knife from his pocket, cut the edge of the lining and put two fingers inside. He felt a packet which he gently removed. It contained what looked like a quarter pound of pure salt. Five minutes later he had removed three other similar packets, one from the same side of the helmet and two from the other. He could feel his heart beating faster and faster as he ran his hand over them stacked together on the table. So this was how Ramirez did it. There was no point in opening them because he had no idea what heroin should feel or taste like.

'Can I help you, Mr Rye?' He wheeled round like a child caught with his hands in a forbidden packet of sweets.

The figure of Henri was framed against the door but the voice did not sound like that of the head lad. Nor was it. Pushing him to one side Inspector Albert Renard strode forward. 'We thought you might come and collect your property. You are under arrest. Come with me.'

Chapter 15

Not surprisingly, Alistair missed Claudia's first night. When he telephoned that afternoon from Deauville police station, her reaction had been disconcerting. Apart from her understandable disappointment that he would not be there to see her first-ever appearance before a paying public, she was angry that he had managed to get himself into such a mess. If now was the time for sympathy and support he did not feel waves of either coming down the line from New York. There was even a brief moment when he sensed that she now suspected that he might after all be involved in drug smuggling and that his discovery of Ramirez's heroin hoard was not just accidental. Their conversation ended with Claudia reluctantly agreeing to fly over at the weekend to see him, and to help if necessary in his application for bail. As Alistair

was all too aware, the chances of his being released
from custody now depended on the skill of Maître
Pression as an advocate and more importantly on
whether he was to be charged with Ramirez's
murder as well as with conspiracy to import and
export unlawful drugs.

The complacent smile on Inspector Renard's face
during the journey from Chantilly to Deauville
had left Alistair in no doubt that as far as he was
concerned his inquiries were at an end. Maître
Pression, who had immediately driven down from
Paris to represent him, confirmed that the inspector was cock-a-hoop, pressing the examining magistrate to charge Alistair forthwith. After hearing
from the maître, the magistrate had postponed his
decision until the following day. Now all Alistair
could do was to lie on his bed in his cell and wait for
the morning to come. He knew it was essential
that he should obtain his freedom because without
it he had no chance of finding out who had really
killed Ramirez. The police plainly had no intention of looking any further, and whilst he did not
doubt for one moment that Claudia would give
evidence for him at a trial, it was an ordeal he
would willingly forego for both their sakes.

He was made to stay in his cell until midday,
when a grim-faced Maître Pression came to see him.

'Monsieur, things are bad, but, I'm happy to say, not yet catastrophic. The magistrate has decided that you are to be charged with certain offences concerning the possession and smuggling of heroin. At the moment no final decision has been made in relation to the Ramirez murder and this is because, as I was able to point out, your wife has given a statement which corroborates your story and as yet no one from the French police has even seen her to challenge it. I have offered to bring her here voluntarily to give a further statement. Is that all right?'

'Yes, of course. I spoke to her early yesterday evening and she agreed to come over this weekend. Are they going to give me bail?'

'Yes, but the conditions are very harsh. They require a security of 5,000,000 francs and an undertaking that you will report to this police station every two weeks.'

'But that's ridiculous! How can I, when I live in America?'

'Otherwise they will take your passport away. Will Mr Morrow put up the money?'

'I simply don't know. There's certainly nobody else. I just hope he doesn't start believing there's something in all this – then I'm done for.'

'Was your wife sympathetic when you called?'

'Barely. She gave the impression that it was extremely tactless of me to go and do this on her first night. There are times when I think she has no idea of my predicament. Or else she's choosing to ignore it in the hope it'll go away.'

'I hope it is neither. At the moment she is the most important person in your life, and I am not talking about love. In a way, you see, she holds your destiny in the palm of her hand,' continued the lawyer, dramatically holding out his hand to emphasise his point.

'Do you think they'll charge me for this murder at some stage?' asked Alistair nervously.

'Do you want an honest answer?' replied the lawyer. Alistair nodded.

'Then yes. Renard is gradually wearing down the magistrate and with their latest bit of information, that is, apart from catching you with the drugs, they are even more confident.'

'What latest bit of information?'

'Didn't I tell you? I'm sorry, but my mind has been so occupied with the application for bail. Two friends of Ramirez have come forward and said they had arranged to meet the jockey at his villa at 8.30 on the evening he disappeared. There was no sign of him when they arrived there and no reply when they phoned throughout the evening. As far as Renard is concerned, that ties in with the

196

murder having been committed earlier in the evening, and more precisely at 6.35 at your villa.'

'I've told you Ramirez left my place alive.'

'I know, my friend. Let us hope the jury believes you as I do.'

'Suppose I am charged; when will the trial take place?'

'At the moment the courts are very congested. I would say the end of June, early July. That makes you smile, Mr Rye?'

'Well, at least that means I can see one last Derby and go to my last Royal Ascot!' joked Alistair.

'You English are all mad, but I admire your sense of humour. I must now leave for Paris. Will your wife be able to bring a banker's draft with her from America?'

'Hopefully, if Mr Morrow is prepared to put up the money. Will you be here on Saturday to see Claudia?'

'Most certainly. If you want, I can drive her down from Paris. I want to see you are granted bail and freed before she gives any statement. If by some chance she makes a bad impression, we don't want our friend the inspector arguing that bail should no longer be granted.'

'Can I leave the country straightaway, then?'

'Why not? There is a flight that afternoon to

London. Do you have any more business to conduct there?'

'There is one small matter which, after what's happened, I now think I want to handle personally.'

The French lawyer discreetly chose not to inquire what that small matter was and instead shook Alistair by the hand and wished him well until Saturday.

It was clear from her harassed expression that Claudia was still angry with her husband. As soon as they were alone in his cell she gave full vent to her feelings.

'Alistair, how can you do this to me? You know how much this part means to me, and after your phone call I was hardly in any condition to go on stage. I've had to let that bitch of an understudy do the part tonight.'

Alistair could hardly believe his ears. This was a whole new side of his wife's character, and he didn't intend to take it on the chin.

'Hold on a moment,' he said. 'Of course I'm sorry about your play but it's not exactly my idea of fun to be cooped up in a French jail facing the prospect of a trial for something I've never done and if that goes wrong a long term of imprisonment. And that's just for the drugs side of it. If I get done for murder I'll be an old man when I'm released. And you worry about missing one bloody performance of your new play!'

Claudia continued unappeased. 'What the hell were you doing at Etienne's yard in the first place? You knew he had come over to New York for the first night.'

'I just wanted to find out from his head lad what time he'd returned from Deauville that day. If *I* didn't kill Ramirez someone else did, and Amy thought that I ought at least to treat Etienne as as much a suspect as anybody else.'

'That girl again!' Claudia was now beginning to sound hysterical. 'You only met her a week ago, and look at the mess she's already got you in. First it was Eddie James, and now this. What kind of hold has she got over you, Alistair?'

'What do you mean? She's a solicitor, and from what I've seen a very good one at that. Look, Claudia, I need help at the moment and with you doing your acting . . .' Alistair regretted his remark as soon as he had made it.

'My acting?' she screamed. 'So that's it, is it? You never wanted me to have a career of my own and having made a mess of yours, you now can't bear me having a chance to do what I want to do.'

'That's simply untrue and you know it.'

'There's no need to shout, Alistair. You and I are

going to have to have a long chat about our future when this is all over.'

'What do you mean by that?'

'Exactly what I said. I've seen the last five years of my life thrown away and I have absolutely no intention of it ever happening again.'

Before Alistair could press her further the cell door opened to reveal Maître Pression and a glowering Inspector Renard. The latter addressed Alistair in a tone of voice which barely hid his contempt.

'Monsieur. The formalities are completed and you are free to go, for the moment at any rate. Please ensure that you report in two weeks' time to this police station. As for you, Madame, I would be grateful if you would follow me so I can take a statement from you. Goodbye, Monsieur, until we meet again.'

He turned and waited for Claudia at the threshold of the cell. However, Maître Pression politely but firmly closed the door in his face and addressed his client.

'I'm very pleased that Monsieur Morrow came up with the money. There is a taxi outside to take you to the airport where a ticket is waiting. I will stay with your wife while she is interviewed and then take her back to Paris. Good luck, Monsieur, and please, please be careful. It is in my experience a dangerous habit to be found too often at the scene of the crime.'

The plane from Deauville landed an hour later at Gatwick. On the journey Alistair felt increasing resentment towards Claudia and her wholly un-sympathetic attitude towards him. He only hoped her ill humour did not spill over into the statement she was giving to Inspector Renard. He wondered anxiously how he could get in touch with Amy, who had so far shown a certain reluctance to give him her home telephone number. The other person he wanted to contact was Willie Grange, to see if the lads had made any progress in 'interviewing' Hassan's bodyguard. He hoped that they hadn't done, as he now wanted to be present at the inter-view himself. His desire for revenge on at least one of his enemies had usurped any notion of playing fair.

Having passed through customs, he was happily surprised to be greeted by both Amy and Willie. They made a curious pair, the tall attractive solicitor in jeans and beside her the small but perfectly formed jockey in a suit which must have cost five hundred guineas from a West End tailor. Willie always did pride himself on his dandy appearance, and expensive suits and fast cars were all part of the image of the successful jockey.

'What the hell are you two doing here?' asked

Alistair, shaking Willie warmly by the hand and touching Amy on the arm.

'Maître Pression telephoned yesterday from Paris and since I got you into this mess the least I could do was come and meet you when you set foot on English soil again. Willie here called yesterday about seeing Hassan's bodyguard, so I suggested he came along. And here we are.'

Willie grinned enthusiastically and grabbed Alistair's case.

'And tonight we've got a little visit arranged,' he added with a twinkle in his eye.

'Yes,' continued Amy. 'We think that Hassan's man has been staying at home for the last few days and Willie and his friends were planning to visit him tonight when the pubs close. I've managed to get hold of a photograph of him, just to make sure he's the right one.' She handed Alistair a black and white mug shot. 'Is that him?'

'Yes, that's one of the men that attacked me at the hotel. In fact, he's the one that held the pliers. He was also with Hassan at the casino. What did you say his name was?'

'Jacques Tissot. Certainly no beauty, and I somehow don't think that scar on his cheek is a birthmark.'

* * *

At ten thirty that evening Alistair found himself
with Willie and three of the 'lads' breaking into a
flat on the twentieth floor of a tower block not far
from the Elephant and Castle. Despite her insis-
tence that she did not want to know what went on,
Amy had nonetheless driven Alistair and Willie
down there, and was now waiting in the car a
couple of streets away. Breaking and entering was
a new venture for Alistair, but for a man accused of
murder and trafficking in heroin, it did not even
interest his conscience. Until he met the lads in
the flesh, he hadn't believed they really existed
and since Willie made no attempt to tell him their
names or encourage conversation, he was none the
wiser as to who they were and what they really did
for a living. One was not a great deal bigger than
Willie, whilst the other two were just over six feet.
The ease with which the small one opened the
door to Tissot's flat certainly suggested a general
familiarity with locks. Once inside in the darkness, two took up positions on either side of the
front door whilst Willie and the lockbreaker hid
behind the sofa. Alistair, imitating Hassan, sat on
an armchair in the sitting room on to which the
front door opened. They had been waiting for what
seemed hours when shortly after midnight a key
turned in the lock. As the burly figure of Tissot

came through the door, he instinctively reached out with his left hand for the light switch. Instead, just as Alistair had done only ten days earlier, he found the contours of a human face. Before he could react, he had been grabbed from behind and pushed into the middle of the room. The light went on to reveal Alistair sitting in the armchair smiling at him.

'Good evening, Mr Tissot. A slight change from the last time we met.'

The Frenchman struggled in an attempt to break free but both his arms were held firmly behind his back in a half-nelson. By now Willie and the locksmith had surfaced from behind the sofa and had begun to tie his hands and feet with some rope brought along for that very purpose.

'What do you want, you bastards? You'll never get away with this,' shouted Tissot. 'Hassan will skin you alive.'

'Shut up and listen.' Alistair could scarcely believe it was his own voice speaking. 'I've had enough of you scum. I've come here for some answers and I've no intention of leaving till you talk.'

'Get stuffed!' answered Tissot and the accompanying spittle which hit Alistair in the eye brought back memories of Ramirez. He responded by kneeing Tissot in the crutch.

He waited until he had recovered his breath before continuing: 'Now: did your master pay Ramirez to pull that race at Deauville?'

'Why don't you ask him?'

Alistair kneed him again, and then again just as he came up for air. 'Who killed Ramirez?'

Tissot's response was to try and butt his interrogator in the face, but Alistair swayed back in the nick of time.

'Do I take that to be an admission?'

Tissot burst out laughing. 'You don't take it to be anything. You're going to regret this!'

By now Alistair's blood was up. 'I hoped you might see sense. Clearly I was mistaken. Willie, open that window over there, will you?'

The jockey duly walked over to the window on the other side of the room and opened it. Alistair then signalled to the lads to pick Tissot up and carry him across the room towards it. The next minute, the Frenchman was dangling outside, head first, in mid-air, looking down at a drop of over two hundred feet.

'Now,' said Alistair, beckoning one of the lads over to help him grab hold of his legs, 'have you had a change of mind yet?' There was no response from the Frenchman. 'All right then, *au revoir*.'

Tissot agreed to talk just as Alistair and the lad slackened their grip. They hauled him back into the room and sat him on the sofa, still shaking with fear. 'Right,' said Alistair. 'The answers, please.'

'I don't know whether Hassan paid your jockey to pull that race, but it wouldn't surprise me. He likes to win, whatever the cost. All I do is what I'm told.'

'Did you kill him?'

'I swear to you I had nothing to do with it. That evening after the race Hassan sent me and a couple of others over to Ramirez's place to get some money back and to rough him up a bit. That's all we were told to do.'

'What time was that?'

'About nine o'clock?'

'And what happened?'

'He wasn't there, was he? So we went back to the hotel and told Hassan.'

'And where was he, all this time?'

'At the hotel, in his room.'

'How can you be so sure?'

'Because he had a couple of tarts in bed with him. All right?'

'And what other attempts did you make to find Ramirez?'

'A lot over that following week, but no one knew where he was. That's it: it's the truth.'

Alistair believed that it was, unfortunately.

Sadly, it now looked like he could cross Hassan off his list of suspects.

'All right, I believe you. Just remember that two can play at your game and next time my friends will not be so sympathetic.' He turned to the others. 'Shall we go?'

They left Tissot tied up and wriggling on the sofa as they made their way quickly to where their cars were parked. Willie and Alistair walked ahead together.

'Christ, Alistair,' said Willie, 'for a terrible moment I thought you were going to let him drop.'

'I know. Thank God Tissot didn't realise I was only joking.'

Willie and the lads headed back to Newmarket whilst Alistair and Amy drove over Westminster Bridge and turned left down the Embankment. In the flurry of activity Alistair had forgotten to book a hotel room and since it was now past one o'clock in the morning he was unlikely to find anywhere to take him for the night. Amy kindly offered to put him up and he didn't need any persuasion to accept. After three nights in a hard bed in a police cell he could hardly wait to lie down on a well-sprung mattress again.

Her small but comfortable flat was just off the King's Road in Chelsea. She told Alistair to make himself at home in the sitting room whilst she rustled up some coffee and eggs and bacon. On the mantelpiece were photographs of what Alistair took to be her parents, a handsome couple with her father sporting a military moustache and a red well-lived face. A large collection of watercolours adorned the walls and the whole room had a homely atmosphere which immediately made him feel relaxed and easy. Its unpretentious style reflected Amy's innate self-confidence. Alistair wandered over to the bookshelves on either side of the fireplace and looked through Amy's collection. There were a large number of detective stories, with Dick Francis and George Simenon's Maigret featuring high on the list, and a variety of works by women authors, ranging from Margaret Drabble to Barbara Taylor Bradford. Pride of place, however, was given to a set of *Timeform* annuals dating from 1952. Alistair was flicking through the pages of the volume for his last year of training when Amy returned with a tray in her hands.

'I was just admiring your collection,' said Alistair. 'Brings back memories, reading about my old runners.'

'They're good, aren't they? My father gave me the earlier ones as a graduation present, which horrified all my friends but delighted me. Since then I've kept up the collection. Come and have some food before it gets cold.'

Eggs and bacon had never tasted so good. Dangling thugs out of windows was a totally new experience for Alistair, and he now looked back on the evening's escapade with a certain disbelief at his own performance.

Amy interrupted his reverie.

'All right then. What happened?' She had refrained from asking any questions on the journey home.

Alistair made a clean breast of it. When he had finished, she shook her head in amazement.

'What if you had dropped him? With his hands and feet tied together you could never have claimed it was an accident.'

'Don't tell me. The idea came to me on the spur of the moment and I think even the lads were pretty shocked at the suggestion. Still, it worked, for what it's worth. We now know Hassan is in the clear, so it's beginning to look more and more like Stride. I no longer know whether I'm pleased or not.'

'Or Etienne. We can't rule him out. We still don't know what he did between the race track and returning to Chantilly. How long a drive is that?'

'Let me think. It's about two hours on the motorway from Paris to Deauville without driving like a maniac, and I suppose that Chantilly is half an hour or so less.'

'Therefore if Etienne arrived at his stables at 10.30 he could easily have murdered Ramirez after he had seen you, dumped him on his way to the motorway and been back nicely in time to see Philanderer to bed. It's possible then, isn't it?'

'But unlikely.'

'I don't agree. What's more, just remember where they found the heroin. Did you enjoy that?'

Alistair had devoured his food and was now sipping a cup of fresh coffee. 'It was delicious. Thank you. I don't know where I'd be without you at the moment.'

'In New York watching your wife treading the boards. Before you ladle out the gratitude, just remember whose idea it was for you to visit Etienne's yard.'

'Come on, that's not your fault.'

'It is in a way. I shouldn't have insisted on telling the Deauville police you were coming over, but at the time it just seemed sensible.'

'That's the trouble with playing by the rules. Racing taught me that's the one way not to beat the handicapper.'

Amy laughed and Alistair again felt a sudden impulsive desire to take her in his arms and kiss her. She seemed to sense this too, as she stood up rather suddenly and said that she would show him his room.

'And tomorrow I want you to go back to New York. You've got to get back into your normal routine for a while, with your work and so on. I'll keep on making inquiries into Stride's background and see if I can dig up anything about this Tucker person. You'd better make your peace with both your wife and Morrow.'

'You're right. Try and act normally, is what they always say in the films.'

'And one other thing. Keep an eye out for Hassan or his henchmen. I don't somehow see them taking this evening's entertainment in the right spirit.'

Chapter 16

Alistair returned to New York to a chilly reception from Claudia, who had flown in earlier that day from Paris. She refused to discuss her interview with Inspector Renard save to say, somewhat sardonically, that she had told him everything Alistair had told her to say. Alistair saw no point in reminding her that all she was required to do was to tell the truth, as at the back of his mind he remembered Maître Pression's remark that Claudia held his future in the palm of her hand. Now was clearly a time for rapprochement rather than antagonism, but her present hostility did not make that task any easier. He hoped that Morrow at least would be more sympathetic when he went into the office the following morning. Apart from having had a week off work, he had asked a lot of his employer, both financially and in terms of trust, and it was essential that he continued to retain his confidence. Dismissal now would be the final straw as far as Claudia was concerned.

Happily Morrow could not have been more understanding. Alistair decided it was essential to make a clean breast of it and tell him everything, up to and including the incident with Tissot on the Saturday night. The only detail he omitted to mention was that Tucker, the name of Stride's co-director, was also Claudia's maiden name. As far as he was concerned, that had to be put down to coincidence. The American was full of optimism and made it clear that he was in no doubt that Alistair would be acquitted on the drugs charge if it ever came to trial. He was, however, dismissive of the notion that Etienne could in some way be involved with Ramirez's death.

'That English lawyer of yours has a vivid imagination. Etienne would be terrified to pick up a knife, let alone use it. Nope, my money's on Stride or the Mafia.'

'I agree it's unlikely,' replied Alistair, 'but at the moment I still don't know what he was doing between the races and getting back to his stables. If he had an alibi, we could cross him off our list.'

'Have you asked him?'

'Not yet. My attempts to find out behind his back have proved expensive enough already. Have you any suggestions?'

Morrow pressed a button on the intercom system on his desk and spoke to his secretary.

'Would you get me Mr Lafayette in France, please?'

With a broad grin on his face he looked across his desk at Alistair. 'We Americans prefer the direct approach.'

The phone rang and he picked it up. 'Hello, Etienne. Everything all right?'

There was a two-minute pause whilst the Frenchman set off on an excited monologue. At last Morrow managed to interrupt: 'I agree it's terrible about Alistair. Yes, yes, you were right about Ramirez. Will you listen a moment? I've Alistair here with me and he'd like to know what you were doing the night Ramirez disappeared.'

Alistair winced at the bluntness of the question, and judging by the audible shrieks of outrage coming down the line, Etienne was also unamused.

Eventually Morrow put the phone down and spoke to his racing manager. 'That guy really knows how to bang on. He says that he left the course at six o'clock and stopped off on the autoroute for dinner on the way home.'

'On his own?'

'He didn't say he had anyone with him.'

'So he could have done it?'

'Theoretically, but can you really see Lafayette loading Ramirez's body into the boot of his car and dumping it in a cow shed?'

'No more than I can see myself doing it, but in my case the police don't regard it as in the least unbelievable. What do I do next?'

'In my opinion, get on with rest of your life. Leave it to the lawyers to sort this one out for the moment. When are you going to see Claudia's play?' Morrow obviously noticed that Alistair's reaction was less than enthusiastic. 'You're not having trouble, you two, are you?' he asked.

'No, well, at least I hope not. All this business has put a terrible strain on her and quite frankly I don't feel I'm getting all the support I deserve.'

'Don't worry, it'll pass. This is a big time in her life and maybe she's seeing things a little out of perspective. If you want my advice, Alistair, be patient and everything will come good again.' Alistair just about managed a half smile; he was beginning not to share his boss's confidence on this particular issue.

'Well, when are you going to see the play, then? The first night was excellent, and do you know something? Claudia really is a brilliant actress.'

'I'm going tonight. Do you really think it's got any chance of moving to Broadway?'

'I don't know much about these things really,

but from what she tells me the backers are more enthusiastic than ever, so maybe we'll see her name in lights next year after all.'

Alistair rose to leave. 'I must do some work. Have you made up your mind what to call your Nijinsky colt?'

The American smiled. 'How about Riding High?'

Love Betrayed was playing in a converted barn at the bottom of First Avenue. Alistair was surprised to see that the theatre was full. The audience contained a mix of arty types and well-attired affluent-looking couples. Scanning the glossy programme, it really did look like the producers, Come Tomorrow Productions, were going to see a return on their investment. The expectant buzz before the curtain rose reflected the good reviews the play had already received in the press and Alistair noticed that the man sitting beside him in the house seats had a pencil and pad in his hand. Either a critic or Broadway impresario, he surmised. The plot was depressing and brutal in its analysis of human emotions and motives. It could hardly be described as Alistair's idea of an evening out, but he had to admit that from the moment she walked on to the stage, Claudia held the audience captive with the power and credibility of her performance.

Playing the role of a woman who was having an affair with the husband of her best friend, she succeeded in capturing the audience's sympathy for her behaviour, even though it was the friend who had been betrayed and was now dying. The man beside Alistair wrote copious notes during the scene when Claudia broke down and confessed to her friend that she had been lying to her all along. For some reason Alistair found himself unhesitatingly forgiving both her infidelity and treachery. The enthusiastic applause at the end showed that he was not alone in his judgement.

Over the next few weeks Claudia buried herself more and more in her acting career and, being overwhelmed with offers, even took on the services of an agent whose offices were somewhere off Madison Avenue. Working every evening except Sunday and reading for parts in the day, she and Alistair saw less and less of each other. He realised that far from drawing them closer together, the impending drugs trial had become a barrier between them. His fortnightly trips to France had continued uneventfully up to Christmas, although the French police treated him with the utmost contempt. Drug dealers come just above child molesters in the popularity stakes. He telephoned Amy regularly on the pretext of finding out whether she had turned up anything on Stride. Although she was always friendly and supportive, she had little to report. Her own inquiries had drawn a blank and on an even more depressing note the police had decided that Eddie James had committed suicide and that the bruises on his arm were self-inflicted.

It was early January when he received a phone call from Maître Pression, asking him to come and see him in Paris before reporting as usual on the following day at Deauville. The anxious tone in the lawyer's voice made Alistair feel uneasy, but the Frenchman refused to be drawn over the telephone. Plainly there was bad news ahead, and Alistair racked his brain to think what could have been discovered now to incriminate him even further. Inspector Renard had so far mentioned nothing about the Swiss bank account but Alistair knew that it could not have been forgotten; whilst he slept in New York, the irrepressible and deter-mined policeman would have been busying away at his goal, slowly but surely building the case against him.

It was just as he had feared. Maître Pression barely waited until he was seated in his office before launching into the bad news.

'I'm afraid that tomorrow you will be charged with the murder of Jose Ramirez. The examining magistrate has, with Renard's assistance, completed his investigations into this whole affair and is now prepared to institute proceedings.'

'But what about Claudia's statement?' retorted Alistair. 'As I hadn't heard anything, I assumed they were satisfied.'

The lawyer shook his head. 'It's true she gave a statement – as you know, I was there at the time – which accords with what you say happened, but it's not so much what she said but how she said it. Do you understand? She was, let us say, diffident, as if it had all been rehearsed, as if she was giving a performance. It didn't live.'

'But it's the truth!' cried Alistair, banging his fist on the desk in front of him. 'And she bloody well knows it is.'

'Calm down. Now is the time for strong nerves. For your sake I just hope she is more convincing at the trial, because at the moment there is a real chance she will be disbelieved. In France, you see, we *expect* a woman to lie for her husband. It is perfectly acceptable and when he is convicted everyone says bravo to her for standing up for him.'

'Have they dug up anything else about me? I wouldn't put it past the old truffle hound.'

'Just one other thing which has finally made up their mind. They have found out about Jean

Gerard. They know it's the name of a horse you once trained – I think that French trainer friend of yours told them – and the Swiss bank have confirmed that the account was opened just over a year ago, shortly after you began travelling to Europe for Morrow, and Ramirez started riding for you. Who else but you would have thought of that name? They reckon you used to bring the heroin in with you and hand it over to the jockey for redistribution. All very simple.'

'But I never brought anything with me into the country except my clothing and some extra cash for Ramirez from Morrow.' Alistair had stood up and was frantically pacing round the room.

'Monsieur Rye, please sit down, you are making me feel nervous. Of course I believe you, but as your lawyer I'm under a duty to point out the case against you. Your problem now is trying to prove a negative.'

Alistair shook his head and swore under his breath. 'That's just it. How can I prove I wasn't carrying anything?'

The next day they drove to Deauville together. Maître Pression appeared anxious not to keep the police waiting, as he kept his foot flat down on the accelerator throughout the trip; they made the journey from the centre of Paris very comfortably in under two hours. Alistair felt a curious mixture of fear and relief; fear because of the fate which might befall him, yet relief because the sword of Damocles which had been hanging over him for the past three months had at last fallen. They were greeted by Renard and the examining magistrate and, to their joint credit, they did the whole thing with a certain style. Alistair was treated politely, almost deferentially, and anyone who was watching without hearing the dialogue might have thought he was being interviewed for a top management job. Instead he was being charged with murder.

His main concern now was to retain his freedom until the trial, and, once again thanks to the persuasive powers of his lawyer, he was not remanded in custody. However, the price of freedom was on this occasion a good deal more onerous. He was to surrender his passport and to report every day to the police in Paris. Even that would not have been sufficient, had not Maître Pression also undertaken to put Alistair up in his own home as an additional guarantee that he would not abscond. After much debate it was decided that since the drugs had been discovered in Chantilly, the trial would take place in the Palais de Justice in Paris in early July.

Claudia took this latest bit of news with almost

callous indifference. At least she was still prepared to come and give evidence, although she wouldn't let him forget that doing so would 'interfere considerably', as she put it, with the second week of her play, which was in fact transferring to Broadway at the end of June. Morrow was, as ever, a brick. As far as he was concerned, Alistair could just as easily run the equine empire from France as from New York, and he even authorised him to rent an office in Paris to use as his temporary headquarters. Alistair was greatly heartened by his support, and indeed by that of one or two of his friends in the racing world. When the news of his arrest and charging broke in the English press there was an initial surge of interest from racing journalists, but after a week or so it died down, and then his real friends could be counted. Of course he only needed one hand to do so, but in a world where failure is an orphan and success has a thousand fathers Alistair knew to expect little else. At least in the forefront of them all were Willie Grange and Amy.

Sadly Etienne was not one of the special few. After Morrow's phone call he could hardly bring himself to talk to Alistair, and did his best to make him uncomfortable whenever he visited Chantilly. There was no doubt that he had come to regard Alistair as an embarrassment; he was probably already planning on who should replace him when he was convicted. Once or twice he even hinted that the honourable thing to do was to retire now. He felt that Alistair's mere association with Morrow's equine empire could adversely affect its bloodstock value. As far as Alistair was concerned, that was a novel argument, and one which he had every intention of ignoring.

His dealings with Morrow's English trainers were a good deal more amicable. Their attitude seemed to be that it was all a vast gallic blunder which would be exposed as such as soon as it came before a court. In the meantime all they wanted to do was to talk about horses, and that was music to Alistair's ears. The best piece of news concerned Riding High. He was being brought along slowly by Toby Hartley, but had already shown immense promise on the gallops. The usual policy with a two-year-old with classic potential was to bring him out in the middle of the summer for his first run and, all going well, try and win one of the big two-year-old races in September or October. However, Morrow had other plans. He loved Royal Ascot and had set his heart on winning the Coventry Stakes. It was therefore agreed that Riding High should have an introductory race at Salisbury at the beginning of June and would run at Ascot two weeks later.

Time now passed quickly and remorselessly, just as it had done at school when Alistair knew that his future depended on his success in summer exams. In March, after Cheltenham, Amy came over for a weekend, and having exhausted the case as a subject of conversation on the first evening, they set about enjoying themselves and exploring Paris together. She never mentioned Claudia and nor did he, but both were always aware of her unbreakable hold over his life, even from five thousand miles away. Alistair now knew that he no longer loved her and that his future, if it lay with anyone, lay with Amy. She for her part never gave any indication of her feelings. His clumsy attempts to make passes were politely ignored as if they had never happened, and the presents he bought her were greeted as much with reproach as with gratitude. He told himself that she loved him, but like a true professional was refusing to cross the line which divided duty from self-interest and emotion.

It was Willie's idea, a week before Royal Ascot, to burgle Stride's offices, and Amy sounded less than pleased when Alistair telephoned her in London for approval.

'Do you want to ruin me?' she shouted down the phone. 'I should never have gone along with you

225

when you visited Tissot, and think what my parents would say if I got caught up in this one? I've no intention of being struck off for you, or anyone else for that matter, Alistair Rye.'

Alistair didn't believe her. 'Don't worry. You're not going to be involved. Willie and his friend the locksmith are going to take a little peep at the mail over the weekend and will show you the contents if there's anything interesting.'

'No they won't,' she replied indignantly.

'Come on, don't pretend you're not interested. What if he's smuggling in heroin? You'd want to know, wouldn't you, just for my sake?'

'Possibly. I'd have to tell the police straight-away, you know.'

'That's fine by me. And now for the good news. Next week, as you know, is Royal Ascot and that demon of the French bar, my lawyer and landlord, has somehow wangled me a day out of France on the condition he comes with me. Claudia has absolutely no intention of coming over, so why don't you join our party? Morrow would be delighted.'

'I'm not sure. I've a lot on at the moment.'

'A day at Royal Ascot and you're hesitating? I must have a wrong number. Go on, grant the wish of a man who may not see this great occasion again, at least not for twenty-odd years.' He did his best to sound imploring.

'All right then, just this once. Is Riding High running?'

'Running and winning. Willie says he was never off the bit at Salisbury and he won there by ten lengths. He's a stone-cold certainty.'

'I've heard that one before! Where shall we meet?'

'I'm going straight there from Heathrow, so we'll have to change into our morning dress in the loo at the airport. Let's meet inside the course, at the Mill Reef bar, half an hour before the first race.'

'That sounds fine. I'll bring my mortgage to put on Riding High.'

'That's the spirit! If I don't call again, see you there.'

Ascot was packed and it was clear that more people than ever had paid their compliments to Her Majesty's Representative. All-grey morning dresses fought with black morning coats and striped trousers to beat Etonian sponge-bags into the queue for champagne, whilst Bond Street jostled Knightsbridge, which jeered at Chelsea, in the battle for the fashion stakes. Somewhere in amongst them all were a clutch of genuine punters trying to get out and watch the horses in the paddock, but on occasions such as these the usual luxury of having a drink, viewing the horses, having a bet and watching the race in the space of twenty minutes would have to be forsaken. In Alistair's case that particular sacrifice was for once easy to bear. To be out of France and free, if only for a day, was a thrill, and when he set eyes on Amy, resplendent in a pink silk dress with matching bow in her hair, his heart leapt in a way it had not done for a very long time.

As far as he was concerned, the first half of the day's racing was only of secondary importance. There was, however, one other thing on his mind. He had not heard from Willie as to whether his visit over the weekend to Stride's offices had yielded any information, and when Amy confirmed that she too had not been contacted he began to fear the worst. Willie had rides for other owners in the first three races and Alistair decided that it wasn't fair to go and pester him in the weighing room, but better to wait until they all met in the paddock before the big one, the Coventry Stakes.

The mere thought of the race rekindled the sensations he had always felt as a trainer when he had a fancied runner; and in this instance he had even greater reason to be apprehensive. Riding High had been bought on his judgement at an astronomical price, and now the day of reckoning had arrived when he was either vindicated or the horse's limitations cruelly exposed. A good win in a maiden at Salisbury was a far cry from victory in the best two-year-old race to date in the season.

They watched the first three races from the stands, and Amy and Maître Pression cheered home the winner on each occasion. The fact that they had ignored Alistair's selections only added to their obvious merriment and Maître Pression insisted on doing a highland jig as he kissed his winning tote ticket. Amy was now full of beans and threatening to go 'nut down' on Riding High. Alistair winced as she furtively looked over her shoulder and, with a huge grin on her face, opened her handbag to reveal a wad of ready money.

'Jesus, Amy,' he said, grabbing her by the arm, 'you're not going to put all that on, are you?'

'And that's not all. I've got another five hundred pounds in the lining of this hat I'm wearing.'

Alistair automatically looked up at the straw boater. 'You're joking?'

'Lawyers never joke, not with the fees we charge. One moment you're telling me to put my mortgage on a horse and the next thing you're going white when I threaten to have just two months' repayments on. Alistair Rye, are you a man or a mouse?'

He was beginning to wonder, and avoided answering by suggesting that they wander down to the paddock, where they were to meet Morrow and then await the arrival of Riding High. Morrow was in his usual ebullient mood, fortified no doubt by large helpings of hospitality from his friends in their box over lunch. They stood in the middle of the vast oblong paddock, with its lush, verdant grass, and waited expectantly for the arrival of their equine hero. Four horses had already arrived and were being paraded by their lads. Next came Riding High. For Alistair it was the first time he had seen the colt in the flesh since that weekend back in October and what he now saw exceeded even his wildest dreams. From a striking yearling he had developed into a strong, beautifully proportioned two-year-old, the muscles on his quarters glistening in the sun at every lazy step he took. He looked and moved like a world beater. In ten minutes they would know for sure.

Willie suddenly popped up out of nowhere in the Morrow colours and playfully doffed his cap to Morrow and Amy. Toby Hartley delivered some last-minute riding instructions, more for effect than any other purpose, as Willie could judge how a race should be ridden better than any trainer. The bell rang for the jockeys to mount and just as he turned to move away, Willie leant over and spoke quietly to Alistair.

'We nicked a parcel from Amsterdam, and it's in the weighing room. The trouble is, someone, I think it was Stride himself, saw us leaving. I'll tell you more later.'

Alistair grinned, trying to pretend to the others that Willie had merely exchanged some idle pleasantry.

They watched him mount and then hurried to the owners' section of the stand to take up their viewing positions.

Amy insisted on rushing off to the bookmakers first, returning panting and out of breath just as the runners were being loaded into the stalls. She squeezed next to Alistair and prodded him in the ribs.

'Mean sods, those bookies. The best I could get was 7 to 4, and even then he didn't say thank you as I handed over the readies. How do you feel?'

'Bloody nervous.'

'And what was that little talk with Willie about? Don't tell me he was giving you the winner of the 5.30 at Pontefract?'

'Nothing so dramatic. He found a little something at Stride's and it's waiting for me in the weighing room. We can go and collect it after the race.' He chose not to mention the jockey's fear that he might have been seen.

'Not with me, you won't. I'll go and have tea with the maître and discuss penal reform'

'Hold on, Amy, they're off.'

Riding High broke slowly from the stalls and the early lead was held by one of the outsiders. Even for six furlongs the early pace was ridiculously fast and Willie wisely chose not to keep up with it. By the time the runners had passed the five furlong pole, Willie was almost as many lengths adrift of the trio who were now blazing a trail in front. Alistair watched anxiously. No matter how confident a jockey may be that the horses in front of him will slow up, it always comes as a relief when their riders begin to throw out distress signals: first the steadily increasing rhythmic movement of the shoulders, and then, as that effort becomes insufficient to maintain speed or position, the recourse to the whip.

With four furlongs of the uphill climb to the winning post remaining, the leading group suddenly started to come under pressure. Without his jockey moving a muscle, Riding High was catching up on them by the yard, and now Alistair became anxious that he might hit the front too soon. He didn't doubt that the horse could make all of the running from this far out, but ideally he would have preferred somebody else to have given Willie a lead for a bit further. He wondered what Willie would do now. Decisions made in split seconds were usually the difference between winning and losing, and that was why the top flat jockeys were always in such demand. There are no real prizes for coming second, even if it is only by the shortest of short heads. Willie had plainly decided not to disappoint Riding High by pulling him back, and as they approached the coconut matting covering the road which crossed the course at that point, he now allowed his mount to range up between the leaders.

A deafening roar came from the crowd, putting its mouth where its money was, and as if in response, Willie gave Riding High a crack with his whip by way of encouragement. The reaction from the horse was immediate, and as far as the bookmakers were concerned, terrifying. Within a second or two a length deficit had become a three-length advantage. Alistair felt a surge of excitement such as he had not felt since his days as a trainer. Now, both horse and jockey seemed to have their ears pricked, and the race at their mercy.

Willie arrogantly glanced over his shoulder at his toiling rivals, and suddenly triumph turned to disaster. One moment he was riding the horse with his hands and heels, the next he was catapulting backwards out of the saddle on to the firm ground behind him. A groan went up from the stands as the backers of the favourite strained through their binoculars to see what had happened. Seemingly unperturbed, Riding High continued riderless towards the finish. Now the race was between two Arab-owned horses and as they flashed past the line together, it was going to be for the judge to separate them. But Alistair's concern was elsewhere – on the sad figure of Willie lying in a heap in the middle of the course. Down below him on the crowded lawn, groups of disappointed spectators were arguing about the incident, whilst the bookmakers on the rails, practical as ever, were shouting out the odds on the photograph.

'What the hell could have happened?' asked Morrow. 'He was going so easily. You don't think Grange fell off deliberately, do you?'

Alistair just managed to hold his tongue. Willie was as straight as the Rowley Mile, and even if he had turned crooked, he was unlikely to have done so in such a dramatic and dangerous manner. As he looked down the course through his binoculars, he could see a motionless body being loaded by stretcher on to a waiting ambulance.

'Where will they take him?' asked Amy anxiously.

'To the hospital across the road if it's half as bad as it looks. I just don't understand it.' He turned to his employer. 'If you don't mind, I'd like to go and see him straight away. Riding High looks to be all right, and if it's any compensation, he would have won that race doing handstands.'

Morrow nodded sullenly. 'Only the jockey chose to do them instead. All right, you go.'

'I'll come with you,' said Amy.

Clutching their hats, they ran as fast as they could through the race crowd and down the road to the hospital. They arrived just as Willie was being stretchered in, and to Alistair's surprise, the jockey was flanked by four policemen. Amy gasped at the sight of the blood oozing through Willie's silk jacket, whilst the course doctor, incongruously dressed in top hat and tails, looked shocked and distressed as he took the young jockey's pulse.

'Excuse me, sir,' said Alistair. 'I'm a very close friend of Willie's. Is he going to be all right?'

The doctor responded with a pained expression. 'It's touch and go, I'm afraid. It's a very nasty wound to the right of his chest and as you can see, he's losing a lot of blood.'

'What a ghastly accident,' muttered Amy, shaking her head dejectedly.

'Accident?' exclaimed the doctor. 'This was no accident. This man's been shot.'

An hour and a half later Alistair and Amy were

pacing nervously up and down the soulless cor-
ridors of the hospital. Inside the operating theatre
Willie was undergoing emergency surgery to
remove a bullet from his chest and without saying
it out loud, they both knew that he was fighting for
his life. It was hard to believe that what should
have been a day of triumph had turned so abruptly
into one of despair. As they had driven in Amy's
car from the racecourse car park, the police had
already cordoned off the approach road, running
parallel to the west side of the course. Although
packed with traffic for hours before racing, it was,
not surprisingly, empty thereafter, and a would-be
assassin, with a telescopic lens, would have a
perfect view of the course and ample opportunity
to pick off his target as the horses came towards
him. In the noise of the crowd there was no chance
of anyone hearing the fatal bullet. By the time the
crime was discovered the assassin could be in his
getaway car and a few comfortable miles away
from the scene of the crime. The advantage of the
unexpected is that it gives the perpetrator an
invaluable head start on those caught unawares.

Alistair kept on looking anxiously at his watch.
He had left Maître Pression behind at the course
with Wayne Morrow, and whatever happened he
had to be on the eight o'clock flight out of England
or he and the lawyer would be for the high jump.

He was reluctant to leave the hospital until they had some positive news, because whilst he realised there was nothing he could actually do, he could at least be present in the same building and will his friend on to survival. Amy, without asking any questions, clearly understood his predicament and as they walked up and down she slipped her arm under his and tried to keep his spirits up.

'It's incredible what they can do today, you know. These surgeons are geniuses and since it's on the other side to his heart there must be a real chance.'

'But did you see the amount of blood he was losing? When I get hold of that bastard Stride!' Alistair clenched his fist in anger.

'Why Stride? How do you know it was him?'

'I didn't tell you, but Willie thought Stride saw him leaving his office. There's obviously something very fishy about that set-up and it now looks like we've found our villains. But what a price to pay.'

'Alistair,' she said excitedly. 'What about the package Willie took? Had you forgotten about that?'

Alistair stopped pacing. 'It's in the weighing room. We must get it before somebody else does. I don't want to leave Willie, but . . . I'll tell you what. Will you drive me back to the racecourse and then

237

come back here and wait and see what happens? I'll phone you from the airport to see if there are any developments.'

'Okay, but I think I'd better come with you when you collect and open the package. If it does contain drugs, you'll need a witness.'

'Shall we tell Pression or Morrow?'

'No,' replied Amy emphatically. 'At least not until we've discovered what it contains.'

By the time they reached Ascot again the racing had finished, and although some stragglers were still drinking outside the bars in the early evening sun, there was a strange and disquieting sense of desolation about the place, that 'after the carnival' feeling. Alistair rushed towards the weighing room and fortunately found one of the jockeys' valets tidying up before leaving.

'I've come to collect Willie Grange's stuff,' said Alistair. 'Is it still here?'

The valet eyed them suspiciously for a moment. 'Hold on, aren't you Alistair Rye?'

'That's me. I'm racing manager to Mr Morrow who owns Riding High. Ghastly business this, we've just been to the hospital where Willie's undergoing surgery.'

'He's going to be all right, isn't he?' asked the valet, with genuine concern. 'Terrible accident, that.'

Alistair was just about to correct him when he felt Amy kicking his ankle. 'Er, yes, terrible. Did you say his stuff was still here? We thought that we could take it back to the hospital.'

'I'm glad you've come, as I wasn't certain what to do with it. Somebody was around here earlier asking about it, but when I asked him his name he said it didn't matter.'

'Really? Was he a tall bloke, in his late forties, with dark curly hair?'

'To be honest, guv'nor, I didn't take much of a look at him. I had enough on my hands with all the jockeys for the last race. It's over here.' The valet walked over to the corner of the weighing room and picked up Willie's suit and other clothing. 'I suppose you want to take his kit bag as well?'

'Might as well. Thanks.' Alistair took the clothing and the bag, a small canvas hold-all.

'Send him my regards,' said the valet. 'You expect this sort of thing in the jump game, but on the flat . . .' He shook his head in disbelief.

They said good-bye and went and found a spot at the top of the grandstand where nobody could see them. Alistair opened the hold-all and brought out a parcel addressed to M and S and labelled 'Fragile'. It was postmarked Amsterdam and was about eighteen inches long and a foot wide and must have weighed about three kilos. By now his hands

239

were sweating and he had great difficulty in ripping open the top which had been sealed with sellotape. At last he succeeded and with a triumphant flourish pulled out its contents. Amy gasped and then roared with laughter. The photographs would have been of great interest to the obscene publications squad at Scotland Yard, but plainly had nothing to do with heroin smuggling. They certainly explained why Alistair had never seen Stride with a girl on his arm . . .

It did not take long for Amy to recover and they soon located Maître Pression drinking champagne and oozing gallic charm to a well-proportioned and slightly tipsy blonde who claimed to have become separated from her party. Morrow had already left for London and now the hour had come for Alistair to return to Paris, and Amy to the hospital. It was the last time they would see each other before the trial began and Alistair desperately wanted to tell her how he felt towards her. Try as he might the words would not come. He just hoped that in two weeks' time he would be free to speak them.

He telephoned the hospital from the embarkation lounge at Heathrow and managed to get through to Amy. The news was good. The bullet had been successfully removed and Willie's condition was now described as stable. Amy was going to stay at his bedside for a couple more hours before going home. For Alistair the journey back to Paris was a great deal more pleasant than it had promised to be a couple of hours previously.

Chapter 17

From the glamour of Royal Ascot to the sombre
dignity of the Palais de Justice, Paris, was a
traumatic leap for Alistair. In the twelve days
running up to his trial he and Maître Pression
went through his evidence again and again until
it had reached the stage that he just longed for
the ordeal to begin. Morrow and Claudia flew in
on the Sunday and they all met for lunch at the
Ritz. It had been agreed that as they were to
be witnesses for Alistair, it was better if they
stayed in the same hotel and that Claudia did
not join him at the lawyer's home on the Ile St
Louis. The prosecution case depended on breaking her as a witness and there was no point in
feeding the notion of collusion between her and
Alistair.

The meal could hardly have been called a

success. Alistair was very much on edge and resented the fact that he was made to feel obliged to Claudia for coming over and missing a week of her play. It had opened on Broadway the week before to ecstatic reviews and her career was now firmly launched into the stratosphere, or at least that was what she told him. She had found no difficulty in adjusting to the idea of fame and stardom and Alistair could not resist a smile at the change in the woman who, only two years previously, could regularly be found covered in horse dung! Throughout the meal he noticed his lawyer watching her intently, looking no doubt for any sign that she might prove unreliable or untrustworthy. Afterwards, as they walked back together to Pression's flat, he pronounced himself to be satisfied.

'Alistair,' he intoned sombrely. 'I will be honest with you. I think your wife has become – how do you say? – a narcissus through all this success, but her *amour propre* will ensure that she gives a winning performance in the witness box. However, after that, I think it may very well be a different kind of lawyer you are needing.'

Alistair smiled at his companion. He had come to accept the inevitability of their parting, and

was no longer pained by its prospect, save perhaps for a certain sadness that what had once
been so good could now be so patently devoid of
substance.

Chapter 18

The court rose as the three judges filed in and took up their seats. In their black gowns and pillar-box hats they sent a shudder down Alistair's spine. To his left sat the jury, five men and four women. Together with the judges they made up a quorum of twelve which would ultimately decide his fate. His eyes wandered up and down the row of impassive faces intent on the notion of fulfilling their civic duty. At least if it had been England he could have tried to guess their backgrounds, their attitudes, but here in Paris he could not hope to see behind the masks. Two of the men were in their late fifties or early sixties, whilst the others he reckoned were all about his age. The women were somewhere in between, and one in particular, wearing glasses and draped from head to toe in black, no doubt in anticipation, looked as if she would have been very much at ease amongst the knitters in the front row at the guillotine. He took a deep breath as the president of the court asked for the charges to be read out, and his plea to be taken. At least the presence of an interpreter ensured that he could follow every word as it was uttered, yet it was only when he heard himself pleading 'Not guilty' that he realised that what was about to begin was truly in earnest.

There was no more time for reflection or fear. The prosecutor rose quickly to his feet and flew enthusiastically into his opening address.

'*Monsieur le President*, members of the jury. The prisoner in the dock, an Englishman, is on trial before you for two crimes which, by their very nature, debase and degrade humanity. On the thirtieth of September last year Jose Ramirez, a jockey born in Mexico but working and living in this country, was found dead in a hut ten kilo-metres outside the beautiful port of Honfleur. He had been murdered, a knife plunged remorselessly through his heart.' He now paused for effect. 'Robbed of that precious right to life which is the cornerstone of our democratic society. And that right is given to all, however great, however low, Frenchman and foreigner. And what is more, it is the inalienable right of a sinner as much as of the citizen who obeys our laws and lives the life of a devout Catholic.

'Because, members of the jury, Jose Ramirez was not a good man. He who had come here to work amongst us betrayed the trust which we had shown towards him. He made money by ruining and corrupting the minds of others. He traded and trafficked in drugs, in heroin. Indeed, such was his venality that he himself became prey to that very addiction which he so willingly and profitably fed in others. And in this venture he was not alone. It is the prosecution case that these drugs were imported from America, and indeed on occasions exported equally illegally out of this country to England, where another jockey acted as the courier for an organisation whose leaders remain unidentified and may well never be. Fortunately, by comparison, the French police have enjoyed greater success in unearthing the identity of the mastermind behind this grotesque and inhuman trade, the self-same person who, the prosecution submits, murdered Ramirez with his own hands on Sunday the 31st of August. I will now tell you how the accused, Alistair Rye, did this.

'That Sunday was the last day of the Deauville racing season. Only two days before, Eddie James, another jockey, had been charged in England with possession of heroin, heroin which he had received two weeks previously from Ramirez. As the accused no doubt realised, if James talked and identified Ramirez it would only have been a matter of time before the Mexican would have then identified the accused, and the downfall of his drugs empire would have taken place. The accused could plainly not afford that, and for those who traffic in death, the death of one more human being is not even worth a prick to their conscience. That evening after racing he invited Ramirez round to his villa, La Cage, situated on the coastal road, leading from Deauville to Honfleur. No one but the accused knows exactly what happened, but we believe that he ruthlessly and mercilessly knifed Ramirez to death, before coolly going out to dinner with his wife and friends, and from there on to the casino in Deauville. And then later that night he drove out and dumped Ramirez's body where it was subsequently found. How can we prove all this, I hear you asking yourselves, and why could a man such as the accused, an Englishman with a respectable background, become involved in such a sordid enterprise? I will tell you.

'Thanks to brilliant detective work, the murder weapon was soon discovered. Although all fingerprints had been wiped from the handle, forensic scientists were able to discover a couple on the cross bar of the knife. Those fingerprints match those of the accused. On his wrist the dead man wore a watch, a present from the American millionaire who employed him, Mr Morrow. That watch had been smashed, and the hands showed six thirty-five, the very hour at which we know that Ramirez visited the accused's home. So what? I hear you saying. That still does not prove the date. But this watch had a date counter and that too had stopped, at the thirty-first. September of course only has thirty days, but in any event that body, as the medical evidence can prove beyond dispute, had been lying in that ditch for at least three weeks. It does not need any great genius to recognise the time and date of the murder – namely 6.35 on the 31st of August last year – and that this watch was smashed as Ramirez fought to defend himself. There are other circumstances, in themselves not conclusive, but in their totality, you will no doubt agree, irresistible and damning. The accused, when challenged, claimed it was Ramirez who had attacked him with a knife and that in the ensuing fight he received cuts to his eye and scratches to his cheek. How curious, you may think, that he did not report this murderous assault immediately to the police, but instead, by his very own admission, went out to dinner with his friends and said nothing about it. Moreover, we know that at seven fifteen or thereabouts he was telephoned by his employer to find out how the meeting with Ramirez, which he had in all innocence proposed, had gone. As far as Mr Morrow was concerned, their relationship was solely that of racing manager and jockey, not that of drug importer and courier and dealer. Not one word is said during this call of any contretemps.

'You may by now be forgiven for thinking that this so-called fight has been invented by the accused after the discovery of the body to explain the wounds to his face, caused almost certainly by the dead man's attempts to defend himself; to explain the blood which has since been found on the suit he was wearing that day, the blood of the dead man, and finally the blood found on the floor boards and on the carpet in the sitting room of that villa – once again the blood of the dead man.

'What, you may wonder, would drive a human being to such acts? The answer, of course, is greed. Two years ago the accused was a ruined man. He had recklessly incurred debts as a racehorse trainer which he was unable to meet, debts amounting to 10,000,000 francs. He sold his stables, all his possessions and took up his job as racing manager in New York. Even then his debts continued to haunt him, and it was then that he hit upon a way to pay them off and become wealthy at the same time. Every month he travelled to France to see his employer's horses and every month he brought with him large amounts of heroin. Inquiries by the American authorities have not yet revealed the source of his supply, but it is clear he earned substantial sums of money. He opened a bank account in Switzerland using the name of a horse he once trained, Jean Gerard, a gesture which no doubt amused him a great deal and one which he never dreamt would be discovered. Large amounts of money were transferred from that account to his accounts in England and soon his debts were repaid, and his future secured. Only Ramirez and the possibility of identification threatened his freedom and fortune, and so Ramirez had to die. It was an act quite simply of cold and callous expediency.

'But even then his greed continued, unabated by the fact that he was under suspicion by the police and already under investigation by the examining magistrate. Thus only two weeks after the discovery of Ramirez's body he was caught red-handed in possession of the dead jockey's hoard of heroin, secreted away, as he no doubt knew, at the stables of the trainer responsible for his employer's horses. It was the last piece of the jigsaw.

'All this is denied by the accused. He has, so he claims, been framed, but by whom and with what motive we have not been told. We do know that his wife, an experienced and able actress, has given statements to the police corroborating his story that Ramirez attacked him at their villa and subsequently left that place unscathed. It is the prosecution case that the accused's wife is lying. In doing so she has perhaps understandably sought to put the interests of her husband and her love for him above the law and morality. It is for you, this court, to judge whether she is to be believed, or rather to be pitied, as the victim of misguided loyalty.

'I will now read the statements obtained by the examining magistrate, Monsieur Boncuit, in the course of his investigation. The makers of those statements are available outside court to give oral evidence if required, either by the court or Maître Pression for the accused.'

The first statement to be read out was that of the pathologist who had examined the body. Death had apparently been instantaneous, and caused by a single knife wound which had pierced the right ventricle of the heart. The clinical neatness of the blow would have meant only a small amount of external bleeding. From the condition of the body, death had occurred between three and five weeks before its discovery. The needle marks on the jockey's arms, which stood out like lights on a runway, indicated that he had been addicted to heroin for about a year. At Maître Pression's request, the pathologist was called to give evidence. He was a tall, confident, well-groomed man in his early fifties. Alistair found it strange to think that his life was spent examining corpses, seeing the macabre and grotesque side of human nature. Maître Pression's style of cross-examination was politeness itself – at least as far as this witness was concerned.

'Monsieur, it would of course be impossible to pinpoint the time of death to any particular day, let alone minute or hour.'

The pathologist agreed entirely.

'And therefore if you ignored the evidence of the watch worn by the dead man, there would be no grounds for asserting that he must have been killed on Sunday the 31st of August or even at 6.35 in the evening or morning for that matter?'

'That is absolutely correct,' came the reply.

'And would it be right to describe the blow which killed Ramirez as being delivered with almost expert precision?'

'Either that, or with a great deal of luck,' was the answer.

'And when you examined the dead man, is it not

right that you also discovered a wound to his bottom lip?'

'It is.'

'And that wound would have bled a great deal, I presume?'

'It would have bled. The precise amount is difficult to quantify.'

'Are you aware of the amount of blood which has been found on the suit of the accused, and the carpet and floorboards of the house where the murder is alleged to have taken place?'

'Yes, I have been given these details by the forensic scientist.'

'And am I not right in saying that this amount of blood is equally consistent with a cut lip, as with this particular type of knife wound to the heart?'

The doctor hesitated before answering.

'I suppose it is possible.'

Maître Pression sat down at that last answer, but no sooner had he done so than the prosecutor rose nimbly to his feet.

'Doctor, if an attempt had been made to wash away the blood caused by a knife wound of this nature, what traces would you expect to remain?'

'That's a difficult question, but I would certainly consider those discovered in this case as consistent with such a hypothesis.'

Alistair's heart missed a beat. It was obvious

that whenever an inference was to be drawn it was going to be to his disfavour.

The next statement was that of the forensic scientist. Details were read out as to how the fingerprints on the murder weapon were subsequently found to have matched Alistair's. Again Pression asked to cross-examine. In contrast to the doctor, the scientist appeared a shy, self-deprecating figure who seemed extremely embarrassed at having to go into the witness box.

Maître Pression adopted a more aggressive approach. 'It is correct that there were no fingerprints whatsoever on the actual handle of this knife?'

'It is,' came the barely audible reply.

'Therefore, whoever stabbed the dead man carefully removed those prints or alternatively was wearing gloves?'

'That must be so.'

'Does it not surprise you, therefore, that he should leave two prints on the cross bar of this dagger?'

'All I can tell you is that they were there. It is not for me to conjecture as to how that happened.'

'These fingerprints were, I understand, that of the thumb and index finger of the right hand?'

'Correct.'

Maître Pression now asked for the knife to be

produced in court. He picked it up with the blade towards him and held the cross bar in his right thumb and finger.

'If I was handing someone back their knife, like this, the fingerprints would be facing the identical direction to those which you discovered on this knife, would they not?' The scientist blushed and seemed reluctant to answer.

'Would they not?' boomed the lawyer.

'Yes,' came the whispered reply.

'Have you ever heard of a murderer who stabbed his victim with a handle?' No reply was called for as the lawyer launched into his next question. 'I presume, although there's no mention of it in your statement, that you looked for fingerprints on the watch of the accused, and its strap?'

'I did.'

'And did you find any?'

'None.'

'What, none at all, not even those of the dead man?'

'Not even his.'

'Do you mean to say that they too had been rubbed off?'

'That is possible.'

'Which, you will agree, is only consistent with someone having removed that watch after the victim was dead and having reset it before smashing it?'

'It is possible, I agree.'

'In fact, not only is it possible, it is almost certainly the only likely explanation, isn't it?'

'That is a matter for the court to determine.'

The lawyer sat down with a thud. This time there was no re-examination.

The next statements to be read were those of the croupier in the casino at Deauville, and the owner of the restaurant in Beaumont en Auge who both stated that they had seen Alistair on the evening of the 31st with a badly cut eye and scratch marks to his cheek. None of this evidence was challenged. They were followed by the statement from Etienne's head lad which dealt with Alistair's fateful visit to the stables and his arrest in possession of Ramirez's heroin hoard. At Pression's request, the head lad was called, and he accepted that it was he, and not Alistair, who had raised the question of the kit which Ramirez left behind. He had nothing else useful to add.

On that unsensational note the court adjourned to the following day.

Chapter 19

That evening Alistair telephoned Amy in London.
She had promised to come over on the Friday of
that week when it was expected that Claudia
would be giving evidence, followed by Alistair
himself. The procedure and approach under the
French legal system was quite different to the
English. Whereas in England all evidence had to
be given orally by the witnesses, in France it was
normal, as had occurred that day, to read out the
statements which had been taken during the
course of the investigation as evidence in themselves. This could lead to a considerably quicker
trial, although it in no way hampered or curtailed
the defendant's right to call such evidence as he
needed to put his case, or for that matter to
summon witnesses whose evidence he wished to
challenge. The overall concern was for the truth

and not necessarily for the conviction of the accused.

Of course, that sounded fine in principle, but at that moment Alistair had little chance of identifying any other likely culprit. His problem was that he alone appeared to have the motive, and he cursed the day he had decided to visit Etienne's stables and do his own bit of private snooping.

Amy at least had heartening news of Willie. He had been taken off the danger list and was making a rapid recovery. Police inquiries had discovered the presence shortly before the Coventry Stakes of an unmarked transit van on the road beside the course. Two men had been observed repairing what appeared to be a puncture and as a result no further thought had been given to their activities.

'Hired by Stride, no doubt,' commented Alistair.

'Not necessarily,' replied Amy. 'How do we know that he even saw Willie that night, and what if he did? He surely wouldn't believe that Willie would try to blackmail him about his sexual inclinations. I've got another theory.'

'Go on.'

'What if the marksman was trying to hit the horse and not Willie, and missed? It's pretty difficult to hit a moving target, and all the more so if the target is a jockey riding a finish.'

'In which case?'

'Who would want to see Riding High dead? Other, that is, than the bookmaker who took my four hundred quid? You guessed it: Hassan. A nice bit of revenge for outbidding him and for our little escapade with Tissot.'

'Have you said anything to the police about this?'

'Not yet. I was waiting to hear your reaction.'

'Go ahead and tell them. He may not have been responsible for the Ramirez murder, but nothing will give me more satisfaction if I'm behind bars than knowing that that fat slob is meanwhile languishing in an English jail.'

'Excellent. I hoped you'd say that, but it may not be that easy to show he was behind it.'

'That should be no problem. Just tell the police to dangle Tissot out of the window of his flat. It's amazing what a bit of fresh air does to his vocal cords.'

The next two days of the trial were devoted to Inspector Renard's evidence and his cross-examination by Pression. The detective was an experienced and polished court performer and answered questions politely and confidently. It was his unshakeable belief that Alistair was the culprit, and he steadfastly refused to be budged from that position. His only obstacle was Claudia's statement, which he had to accept reiterated what she had told the American police when they first questioned her. He dismissed its probative value with a gallic shrug of the shoulders and added that in his view, borne of thirty years of interrogation, she was lying.

'And pray, Inspector,' asked Maître Pression sarcastically, 'what was it in her demeanour or manner which allowed you to form such an impression?'

The inspector took a couple of deep breaths and looked round the crowded court. Eventually his gaze came to rest on Alistair in the dock.

'Quite simply because her statement did not live. It was as if her responses had been programmed. It is my view that this woman speaks from here' – he pointed dramatically to his head – 'and not from here,' pointing equally dramatically to his heart.

After Renard, the prosecution case was something of an anti-climax, but that did not detract from its overall impact. A short statement from Morrow was read in which he gave details of Alistair's employment, the basis upon which he had retained Ramirez, and an account of the Deauville race and his subsequent instructions to

Alistair to give Ramirez his notice. He stated that he had flown to Paris by private plane immediately after the race, arriving at his hotel, the Plaza, at approximately 5.15. He had telephoned Alistair at La Cage from his hotel room at about 7.15 and been given a few details of what had occurred. There had been no mention of any fight or assault by Ramirez and the first he learnt about it was after the discovery of the body. It was right that in September, and after Ramirez's disappearance, Alistair had suggested recruiting a stand-by jockey to ride Philanderer in the Arc de Triomphe, but for his part Morrow had always believed that Ramirez would show up in time to ride in the race. He had had no idea that Ramirez was a heroin addict and rejected any suggestion that Alistair could be involved in a heroin smuggling operation. He knew nothing about any secret Swiss bank account and had never heard of Jean Gerard.

On the face of it the statement was not that helpful to Alistair, and since Morrow had volunteered to give oral evidence on his employee's behalf, Maître Pression informed the court that he wished to reserve his right to question him until later in the trial.

Thursday was taken up with lengthy legal argument as to the admissibility of evidence relating to the Swiss and English bank accounts, which to Alistair's dismay was adjudicated emphatically against him. The scene was now set for Friday and Claudia.

Chapter 20

By agreement Alistair had not tried to contact
Claudia during the trial, and she, like the other
potential witnesses, had been obliged to wait
outside the courtroom to be called. A state of
affairs, he reflected, which was hardly likely to
improve her humour. Since Morrow was to follow
Alistair into the witness box, he at least was in the
happy position of being able to carry on his
business in the meantime from his hotel suite.

Alistair was understandably nervous as he and
Maître Pression made their way to the Palais de
Justice. They had left the lawyer's apartment in
plenty of time and tried to relax by walking around
the Ile de la Cité watching the Parisians going
about their daily routines and the café owners
serving coffee and croissants to the tourists. As
they walked past the magnificent cathedral of

Notre Dame, Alistair felt sorely tempted to pop in and say a couple of dozen Hail Marys. He decided on reflection that not being a Catholic, it might be regarded by the Almighty as a shade opportunistic.

By the time they arrived outside the courts, a large crowd of photographers had already gathered and it dawned on him for the first time that he was the unwitting star in what, as far as the French press was concerned, had become a *cause célèbre*. Or was he? The photographers had never been out in such force before, so maybe it was Claudia they were waiting for. The man whose freedom hangs on the word of the woman he loves is the kind of story which can fill magazines anywhere in the world. He chuckled to himself at the thought of how they would react should the truth be known – that his wife had come to despise him and that their marriage was in tatters! They were about to enter the courtroom when Amy arrived, just as she had promised.

She rushed over and kissed him on the cheek. 'I just wanted to say good luck today,' she said.

'And who the hell is this?' The caustic tone in the voice was unmistakable. With her impeccable sense of timing Claudia had arrived at just the wrong moment.

Alistair pretended to take it all in his stride. 'Ah, Claudia. Allow me to introduce you to Amy Frost, my London solicitor. Amy, this is my wife Claudia.' Amy held out her hand, but Claudia chose to ignore it and instead rounded on her husband.

'I'd have thought you could have left your gallivanting until after the trial.' Before Alistair could answer she waltzed imperiously into court.

There was a hushed and expectant atmosphere as Maître Pression rose to his feet and called the first witness for the defence. The jury, the press, the packed gallery of spectators had all been waiting for this moment and at last it had arrived. Anticipation was writ large on even the judges' faces.

Claudia moved slowly and with measured steps to the witness box. Dressed in black (Alistair recognised it as a designer creation she had bought for his father's funeral the year before) and wearing no make-up for the first time ever in their marriage, her gaunt, drawn appearance conveyed the impression of a woman in torment. Her voice quivered as she took the oath and her first few answers to Maître Pression's questions were barely audible. She spoke of their courtship and the early years of their marriage, of his success as

269

a trainer. She fought back the tears as she told the court of how suddenly one day Alistair had told her they were ruined and they had been forced to sell everything. To Alistair's dismay she chose not to mention that he was the innocent victim of the dishonesty of one of his owners; instead she gave the impression that she had never been told the reason for their financial downfall. He decided to put the omission down to nerves, but it played on his mind as the trial progressed.

She then gave evidence of their move to America and Alistair's work for Wayne Morrow. Finally, with great deftness, Maître Pression brought her to that fateful evening when Ramirez visited them at La Cage. Slowly and without ever looking in Alistair's direction she recited what had happened. Gradually the facts emerged one by one, corroborating Alistair's own version of events, but as they did so her manner of delivery sounded more like an incantation than a sincere rendition of what had happened. The occasional studied pauses only accentuated the impression of a witness who was not telling the truth, let alone the whole truth and nothing but the truth. Alistair turned round from his position in the dock and looked at Amy sitting three rows behind him. Her face was a picture of hatred and anger as she stared at Claudia. Amy knew, and now he knew too.

When Maître Pression had finished, the prosecutor rose quietly and confidently to his feet. He looked across the court at Claudia and for what seemed an eternity said nothing. He then spoke in a firm and powerful voice which echoed round the courtroom.

'Madame, now can we have the truth?'

Claudia bowed her head and in a hushed tone replied, 'But I have told the truth.'

'Then we must start at the beginning again. When you and your husband left England you were penniless?'

'Yes, I've already told the court that.'

'As far as you were aware you had no money in your bank account in England?'

'That's correct.'

'And no money in any other account?'

'We had no other account.'

'Who paid for your apartment in New York?'

'I believe it was Mr Morrow, but my husband handled all our financial affairs.' Alistair jerked his head forward in disbelief. Claudia had always been in charge of both the stable's finances and their own.

'Would you be surprised to hear that your

husband had a deposit account in England with substantial sums in it?'

'But that's impossible. There must be some mistake.'

'Do you know a Jean Gerard?'

'Only a horse by that name which my husband once trained.'

'Were you aware that your husband had opened a Swiss bank account in this name and paid substantial sums of money into it?'

'I don't believe you. We didn't have any money except what Mr Morrow gave us.'

'Have you any idea how your husband could have come by that money, Madame Rye?'

Claudia now looked over towards Alistair for the first time. She was playing the role of the innocent, duped wife to perfection. 'No.'

'When did you first hear about the discovery of Ramirez's body?'

'When my husband telephoned me from Paris.'

'When was that, exactly?'

'I can't be sure. I think it was the day of or the day before the Arc de Triomphe.'

'What state was he in?'

'I can't remember.'

'Come, Madame Rye, it can't be every day your husband telephones with such sensational news. Was he in a state of shock, or even excitement?'

'I'm sorry. I just can't remember.'

'Try, take your time.'

She paused, as she appeared to search her memory. 'He was anxious, nervous. He was shouting.'

'Shouting? But why?'

'He was shouting about what happened that night at the villa.'

'And what did happen that night?'

'I've told you already.'

'You told us you were present throughout the meeting between your husband and Ramirez, and that you saw Ramirez leave, but that's not true, is it?'

'It is, I swear it.' Her voice started to shake.

The prosecutor then picked up the knife with which Ramirez had been murdered. 'Do you recognise this knife, Madame Rye?'

Claudia looked away.

'I said, do you recognise this knife?'

She nodded.

'Isn't this the knife you saw your husband stab Ramirez with that evening at La Cage, the knife he used to destroy the man who had become a danger to his own freedom?'

All eyes turned on Claudia. She was sobbing hysterically and running her fingers through her hair. Alistair suddenly remembered where he had seen this performance before. It was the prelude to

the confession scene in *Love Betrayed*. The bitch.
His heart started to beat much faster. This certainly wasn't the time to let life mirror art.

'Madame Rye,' the prosecutor now shouted
dramatically, 'I demand you answer me.'

Slowly and painfully the words came forth
through the tears. 'He made me . . . made me lie.'
She paused for maximum effect. 'He told me if I
didn't, he would . . . he would kill me.'

Alistair was unable to contain himself. He rose
to his feet and started shouting. 'That's just not
true and you bloody well know it! You double-
crossing little . . .' But before he could finish, the
two policemen guarding him in the dock had
grabbed hold of him and pulled him back into his
seat. For a moment chaos reigned in the courtroom, with the presiding judge shouting irately at
Maître Pression, and the prosecutor thumping
theatrically on the table in front of him at this
latest outrage. Alistair was too angry to care. He
had never hit a woman in his life but if he could
have leapt across the courtroom and put his hands
on his wife's throat he would unhesitatingly have
done so. As he slowly regained his composure he
became aware of Maître Pression looking anxiously at him and imploring him with raised hands
to keep calm. It was the last thing he really felt
like doing. The lawyer wasn't having to suffer the

public destruction of his marriage, to be followed by thirty years of wasted life and solitude in a French prison. He turned round to look for Amy. She was staring at him, her eyes pleading with him not to give in. Reluctantly he nodded to Pression who then rose and apologised to the court for his client's behaviour. Alistair was all too aware that no-one believed the lawyer's client felt the least bit repentant.

That last piece of ritual over, the prosecutor now resumed his questioning. He made no attempt to conceal his smug sense of superiority as he moved in for the kill.

'Madame, you have nothing to fear now. Tell this court the truth about what happened that evening.'

'Alistair came home at about 4.30 from the races. He was in a furious temper. He told me that we were ruined unless he took some action. I didn't know what he was talking about and when I asked him he shouted at me and asked how I thought he had managed to pay off all our debts on the salary he got from Morrow. I had no idea what he meant. He poured himself a drink and then told me what he had been doing, how he had been smuggling heroin into France and using Ramirez as a distributor and courier; that the police had now caught their English contact, and that if he told them about Ramirez, we would then be at Ramirez's mercy. He kept on drinking and I begged him not to do anything stupid, but he was like a man possessed. It was a side of his character I had never seen before, that I never knew existed.' She paused and wept for a few moments.

'And then what happened?' asked the prosecutor.

'The bell rang at about 6.15 and he told me to go upstairs. I went to the bedroom and I could hear them downstairs arguing and shouting. Eventually I could bear it no longer and I went down to try and reason with them. I went into the sitting room and there they were on the floor fighting. Alistair was on top of Ramirez with a knife in his hand. He obviously didn't hear me come in as at that moment he lifted the knife and . . .' She turned away.

'Go on, Madame.'

'At that moment he lifted the knife and plunged it into Ramirez's chest.'

'And then?'

'He got up. There was blood on the sleeve of his jacket and on the carpet which he made me do my best to clear up. He then told me that I was to say nothing to anybody about what had happened and that if we were ever challenged later, to say that Ramirez had attacked him with the knife and he had wrestled it from him and that the jockey had left the house alive.'

'And what happened to the body?'

'That night we went out as we had planned with our friends and then later on to the casino. Alistair had wrapped the body in a blanket and left it behind a sofa in the sitting room. It was the maid's day off and she would not be back until the morning. That night when we returned from the casino we loaded the body into the car and Alistair drove off and dumped it on his own. Ramirez was very light to carry, you see.'

'Madame, why have you not told anyone this before?'

Her whole body shook as she answered. 'Because I was afraid and because . . . because I loved him.'

Alistair just laughed. Love? Claudia obviously loved nobody but herself and now that he had outserved his usefulness he was to be discarded, and in the most dramatic fashion imaginable. A bitch through and through; brilliant and beautiful, but still a bitch.

In the stunned silence which now followed, Maître Pression rose and asked for an immediate adjournment until after the weekend. He stressed to the court that he needed to take his client's instructions as a matter of urgency. The prosecutor, generous in his triumph, indicated that he had no objection, provided that Alistair was kept in custody. The grounds for giving bail, he argued, no longer existed. Pression implored the court to take another view – he would personally vouch for his client's whereabouts throughout the entire weekend and would guarantee his presence in court on Monday. Indeed, his client still maintained his innocence and to flee the country was an act as remote from his mind as it was repugnant to his sense of honour. Somehow Alistair doubted whether anyone in court believed that he had the faintest notion of honour, but his lawyer's speech did the trick and he was allowed to maintain his freedom, perhaps for the last weekend for many years.

Chapter 21

That night the three of them, Amy, Pression and Alistair, dined together in the lawyer's apartment and dissected Claudia's evidence. Not surprisingly the atmosphere was extremely stormy. Amy refused to accept that her sudden change of testimony was anything of the sort.

'Your wife's a liar and if you want my view she's been putting on an Oscar-winning performance since this whole thing began.'

'But why?' said Alistair despondently. 'I thought our marriage was fine until this play business cropped up.'

'Alistair, at times your naivety is breathtaking. They say the husband is always the last to know and you're no exception. Are you sure Ramirez smashed his watch during the fight?'

'I don't remember it happening, but then again it was all over so quickly. It could have happened, I suppose.'

'Who else but Claudia knew that Ramirez came to see you that night?'

'Etienne. I'm sure I mentioned it to him at the races. And Morrow of course.'

'And were you with Claudia for the whole of the evening? I mean, was there any time when she could have telephoned or told somebody what had happened and used that incident with the knife to set you up?'

Alistair thought back on the events of the 31st of August. 'After dinner and whilst I was telling the Donnellys about Stride she went to powder her nose. I suppose she could have made a phone call then, but who to? And then at the casino I caught her talking to Stride after I returned from my meeting with Hassan.'

'How did she appear then? Flustered or what?'

'Not flustered, no. She was certainly being friendly to him. He wanted to give me an ex gratia payment, and Claudia got livid with me when I refused. She wouldn't talk to me on the drive home. I asked her at Newmarket whether she had said anything to Stride about the fight and she denied it.'

'Well, she would, wouldn't she? And after what we've heard today you can't believe a word she's said, the bitch. Do you have a pen handy? I want to make some notes.'

'There's one in my jacket on the chair over there.' Alistair made to get up from the table.

'Don't worry,' said Amy, 'I'll get it. It's in the inside pocket?' She felt inside and brought out a theatre programme.

'What's this?'

'It must be the programme for *Love Betrayed*. I can't have worn this suit since the evening I saw it.'

Whilst Pression and Alistair chatted over a glass of cognac Amy flicked through the programme. Then she startled them by suddenly announcing that she had an idea.

'Alistair, tomorrow you and I are going to spend a night together at the Plaza.'

'What? Have you gone mad?'

'No, I've made up my mind. I'll pay.'

'But Amy,' interjected Pression, 'it's impossible. I have given my word to the court not to let him out of my sight.'

'Then you won't. I'll book two rooms next door to each other. Can I use your phone, Maître?'

'If you insist. But something tells me you're up to

281

no good. I am his lawyer, after all. Are you sure you don't want to share this idea, this plan with me? Is there nothing you will tell me?'

'Nothing.' She grinned at him.

'In which case, young lady, I'm too old to argue!' He raised his glass. 'We must not give up hope. Here's to justice!'

Alistair tried to remember the last time he had heard that toast.

After dinner, and against Pression's advice, he telephoned Morrow at the Ritz. His employer sounded embarrassed and bewildered. He had heard from Claudia what had happened in court and apparently she was now under sedation and police protection in her room. Alistair's protestations of innocence were greeted by silence.

'Are you still prepared to come and give evidence on Monday?' he asked the American.

'But what can I say now? I was in my hotel room at the Plaza when all this happened. Up to now I've only heard one side of the story, but why should Claudia now want to lie in court? I'm sorry, Alistair, but I just don't know how you could have done this to me.'

'But Wayne, I've done nothing. Can't you see this is all a ghastly mistake, that Claudia has told a pack of lies?'

'Why would she want to do that? I asked you in

New York if there was anything wrong between you two, and you told me that it was just a rough patch and that you'd get through it. I'm sorry, Alistair, I've got to say it again. I feel betrayed.'

Alistair realised there was no point trying to reason with him any further. 'You're wrong, that's all I can say. Maître Pression will call you on Sunday if he sees any point in your still giving evidence.'

He put down the phone and went and sat next to Amy on the sofa. 'You probably gathered what attitude he's taking.'

'I'm sorry. It was to be expected, I suppose, but that doesn't make it any easier for you, I know.'

'The price of loyalty. I wish I could say I didn't like him anyway but it wouldn't be true. It looks like I'll be looking for a new job as well as a new wife when this is all over.' He turned towards her and leading with his chin asked, 'Do you think I'll still be attractive in thirty years' time?'

'What do you mean, thirty years?'

'That's when I'll be out of prison, according to the maître.'

They booked into the Plaza Athenée at 5.15 in the afternoon. Maître Pression said he found it a trifle absurd to be spending Saturday night in a hotel in Paris when he lived only a mile or so away, but

Amy told him to grin and bear it and think of the enormous dinner they were going to eat in the restaurant. At this the lawyer patted his ample belly and smiled contentedly.

Alistair for his part had decided to forget about the trial for one night and was feeling extremely excited about the prospect of sharing a room and, he hoped, a bed with Amy. His only worry was that Pression might take his undertaking to the court too literally, and insist on sharing a room with him. Happily it was soon apparent that the lawyer had no such intention, and he waved an affectionate *au revoir* as he was shown to his room. Agreeing to meet in the downstairs bar for an aperitif at 7.30, Alistair and Amy followed the bell boy to their room next door.

They had barely been in their room for five minutes when Amy announced that she wanted to telephone the Normandy Hotel in Deauville. Having obtained the number from the switchboard she dialled it herself and to Alistair's astonishment made a reservation for a room for the first weekend in August.

'What the hell have you done that for?' he asked as soon as she put the phone down.

'Just planning a celebration for us when this is all over,' she replied with a huge smile on her face.

'Thank God you're an optimist. By the way, there's no chance of you giving evidence for me on Monday, is there? You know, something on the lines of how you were passing by La Cage on the evening of Saturday the 31st of August and by chance happened to notice a pint-sized Mexican jockey leaving the house at 6.45 or thereabouts?'

'It wouldn't be any use,' she answered, shaking her head and pretending to take his suggestion seriously.

'Why?' asked Alistair, continuing their game.

'Because Claudia would no doubt go back into the witness box and say she made a mistake and that it was at Ramirez's house that she saw you murder him. The court would regard it as an understandable lapse on her part and hey presto, you're convicted!'

'You're right,' he sighed. 'What do we do next, then?'

'We could always have a bath,' she said with a twinkle in her eye.

'You mean together?'

She smiled and playfully undid the buttons on her blouse. Alistair needed no further encouragement and taking her in his arms he kissed her long and passionately. Thirty years of celibacy was staring him in the face and he had no intention of not yielding to the pleasures of this particular moment. Within minutes they were lying naked on top of the bed and he was doing things to her body with his tongue which had hitherto only featured in his fantasies.

Her reaction was uninhibited and enthusiastic. Her hands gripped his hair feverishly in her excitement, and in his desire to please and tease her he didn't care if she pulled the roots out.

'What about our bath?' she whispered.

'That can wait,' he murmured, as he paused momentarily to look up at her before returning to his labour of love. Gradually he could feel her becoming more and more aroused until finally her body shook as if the devil himself had been exorcised from it. Her response served only to spur him on. Turning her over he licked her body upwards from the tips of her toes to the nape of her neck whilst his left hand played havoc with the rest of her.

Soon she could stand it no longer and implored him to take her. Together their bodies moved rhythmically as one and the room filled with their cries of ecstacy. For those brief moments Alistair knew true happiness and oblivion.

Dinner was a monument to gastronomy and at eleven o'clock they staggered up to their respective rooms. The prospect of making love to Amy again would make it a memorable evening and as far as Alistair was concerned sleep was the furthest thing from his mind. Fortunately Amy was of exactly the same mind and they spent the next few hours in exploring and teasing each other's bodies. It was love-making of a sort which Alistair had never previously experienced. With Claudia he had always gained the impression that it was an act devoted to the celebration of her own sexual desire and that he was just a bit player in the drama. With Amy he sensed the constant desire to please and to arouse and that in turn heightened his ability to reciprocate. He could not remember when they eventually fell asleep, only that he woke up with her head resting on his naked chest.

They met downstairs to check out and Alistair and Pression sat in the lobby whilst Amy walked over to reception to collect the bill. Although they had both offered to pay she still insisted on doing it herself. Ten minutes later she was still there, and Alistair went over to find out what was happening.

'Is there anything wrong?' he asked, as she stood drumming her fingers on the reception desk.

'Nothing to worry about. Go and sit down, I'll be with you in a moment.'

Just as Alistair turned to leave, the receptionist

returned. 'Here it is, Madame, it's on the computer. You made one call to Deauville at precisely 5.25. The number was 546982.'

'Are you sure?'

'I'm quite sure. Look, you can see for yourself. It's here on the print-out.'

Amy grabbed the sheet and looked at it.

'Yes, you do seem to be right, after all. I'm so sorry, but when I just saw a figure for telephone calls on my bill I was puzzled.' She paid by credit card and as they went to collect Pression, Alistair could not help but express his surprise at her behaviour.

'What on earth were you doing? I saw you make that call to Deauville. You can't have forgotten it.'

'It must be my memory. You see, that's what comes of you being such a wonderful lover.' She kissed him full on the lips under the benign gaze of his lawyer.

They were in a taxi on the way back to Pression's flat when Amy asked him if he knew anyone of influence in the Paris police force.

'How about the Commissioner of Police? Is that senior enough for you?' he answered with his usual good humour.

'Not bad, Maître, and how well do you know him?' Amy inquired gently.

'Let's put it like this. He's married to the only one of my cousins I could ever stand and we've even been known to go on holiday together.'

'Perfect! And does your *entente cordiale* extend to his helping you out now and again when you have a problem?'

'It has been known to happen. Do you have something particular in mind or is this just a who's who in the French police force?'

'Yes, Amy,' Alistair now butted in. 'What are you up to? Is this something to do with your antics at the hotel?'

Amy nodded. 'All right, this is my idea. It may not amount to much but you might as well both hear it.'

They had arrived at the flat, and Alistair couldn't even wait to put their case down before asking Amy to come clean.

'It's like this,' she answered. 'In my view we've all been looking at this case from the wrong way round. Let me explain . . .'

Much later that evening, after a number of frantic telephone calls to the Commissioner of Police and a police-escorted tour of all the car-hire firms in Paris, an exhausted Alistair went to sleep, dreaming of freedom with Amy.

Chapter 22

The queue outside the Palais de Justice stretched for over a hundred metres as gaggles of men and women waited for a chance to obtain a ring-side seat at what they hoped would be the final episode in the conviction of the English heroin baron. It was not a description Alistair much relished but *France Dimanche* no doubt felt under little obligation to cater for his sensibilities when reporting the case. There is nothing more satisfying than the trial of a foreigner on a murder charge, particularly when it is a well-bred Englishman.

Claudia was still in the witness box, and it now fell to Maître Pression to re-examine her. Fortunately the inquisitorial nature of the French legal system allowed him to be as hostile as he liked, provided, of course, he had some ammunition to fire. Alistair sat nervously on the edge of his seat, wondering whether his lawyer would adopt an aggressive approach from the outset or seek to lull Claudia into a false sense of security.

The very first question provided the answer.

'Madame, you are a liar!' Pression barked across the court. Even Claudia rocked back in surprise. 'Madame, I put it to you that the story you told this court on Friday was a pack of lies from beginning to end.'

Claudia resorted to her usual bout of sobbing. Pression was unimpressed. 'Usher!' he roared. 'Bring this woman a handkerchief and a glass of water. Madame Rye, please abandon this charade. When did you first decide that the version of events which you told the American police and then Inspector Renard was not in fact the truth?'

Claudia appeared to recover her composure. 'I lied to the police because I was afraid of my husband and because I loved him. I tried to lie to this court on Friday morning but finally, as you saw, I could bear it no longer.'

'Really? You are an actress, are you not, Madame, and a very accomplished one at that?'

'It's for others to say how competent I am. I trained as an actress as a girl but I've only just had my first professional role.'

'Is that the play called *Love Betrayed*?'

'That's right, but I assure you and the court I'm not acting now.'

'Do you remember receiving any phone call that evening at La Cage after you say your husband murdered Ramirez?'

'Yes, I thought I already told the court. Wayne Morrow phoned from Paris to find out what had happened at the meeting between Alistair and Ramirez.'

'And what did you tell him?'

'Hardly anything. How often must I tell you that Alistair made me swear not to tell anybody what had happened? I had to pretend to be my normal self on the phone.'

'But of course you were in a state of terrible anxiety. After all you had just seen your husband murder a man in cold blood, hadn't you?'

'There's no need to put on that sarcastic tone. I felt terrible but I couldn't betray Alistair, I just couldn't.'

'Very touching,' commented Pression, looking round the crowded court. 'So just what drove you to betray him on Friday? Don't tell me it was the ferocious cross-examination of my friend, Monsieur the Prosecutor?'

'No. It was simply the burden of my conscience. I couldn't live my life any more knowing what I know.'

'Even if it meant sending your husband to prison for the rest of his life?'

Claudia looked down sheepishly and played with the pearls on her necklace, the only addition to the outfit she had worn to such effect on Friday.

Pression continued on, unmoved. 'Are you fond of your husband's employer?'

'He has been very good to us.'

'Is that all?'

'What the hell do you mean?' For the first time a hint of the real Claudia was beginning to show.

'Madame, it is my privilege to ask the questions. Did Mr Morrow, for example, encourage you to take up acting again?'

'Yes, he did. He discovered that I had once been at drama school in London and very kindly offered to pay for me to go to acting classes in New York. Our own finances, as you well know, wouldn't have permitted it.'

'And did perhaps Mr Morrow provide the financial backing for your first dramatic role in *Love Betrayed*?'

Alistair was certain that Claudia hesitated, albeit imperceptibly, before replying, 'Not that I'm aware of. I just got a part as an actress. The financial backing is left to the producers. Ask them.'

294

'I may have to, but in the meantime could you just look at this?' Pression handed up the programme which Amy had found in Alistair's jacket. 'Is that the theatre programme for *Love Betrayed*?'

Claudia scarcely bothered to glance at it. 'Yes, for the off-Broadway production.'

'Madame, would you kindly look again, this time on the first page, and read out the name of the producers.'

Claudia seemed extremely reluctant to do so.

'It's right there, Madame, at the top, above the title.'

The words came out very quickly: 'Come Tomorrow Productions.'

'A little slower, Madame, this time. And could you please pause after the word "to"?'

'Come To . . . Morrow Productions,' said Claudia.

'I suppose that's just a coincidence, Madame, is it?'

This time she did not condescend to reply.

'Madame, if I can go back to that phone call. How do you know it was from Paris?'

'Because he told me so.'

'Could it not just as easily have been from a phone box down the road?'

'What do you mean? There were no pips or anything. Ask Alistair; he took the call after me.'

'Please, Madame, you know full well that in France, just as I believe in England now, there is no way you can know whether a call is made from a phone box or a private line.'

'Mr Morrow was in Paris. He said so in his statement. Why don't you ask him?'

'I intend to, Madame. All in good time. At the moment he's waiting outside court to be called. You see, Madame, if you wanted to, and I suggest you did, you could have told Mr Morrow about your husband's fight with Ramirez, about the knife with his fingerprints on it, and what would then be easier for you than to kill two birds with one stone?'

'But why would I want to do that?'

'This time, Madame, I will make an exception, and answer your question. Because you and Wayne Morrow were lovers.'

'It's a lie!' she cried. 'A damned lie.'

'That, Madame, will be a matter for the jury to decide.'

Pression then called Morrow to give evidence. He entered the court as Claudia was taken outside sobbing. Unaware of what had been going on, he looked unperturbed, the picture of respectability in his well-cut dark grey suit. Pression began by asking a few background questions as to his business career, his interest in horse racing and how he had come to employ Alistair.

'Please tell the court, Mr Morrow,' said Pression, 'what your initial impressions were of this young English couple.'

'I liked them both enormously from the outset. Alistair was hard-working and able, and, dare I say it, appeared completely trustworthy. Claudia, his wife, struck me as a very loyal, devoted woman with considerable intelligence and courage. Yes, I can honestly say I thought they were a fine well-matched couple, which makes this whole business all the more unbelievable.'

'You feel betrayed, Mr Morrow?'

'That's an understatement. I thought I'd given Alistair a real chance and I find it hard to believe that he could do this – not just to me, but to murder Ramirez and to use his position of trust to peddle drugs. It's incredible.'

'So you believe absolutely the evidence of Mrs Rye?'

'I have no reason to think that she would lie.'

'You surprise me. She was apparently able to lie to the police when she gave them her statements and to lie initially to this court when she first gave her evidence.'

'But she was afraid of her husband, and what's

more, she wanted to protect him. I can understand that.'

'How would you describe your own relationship with Mrs Rye?'

'I don't get you,' replied Morrow a trifle testily.

'You know: as a father-daughter relationship, or what?'

'I've already told you that I thought highly of her. When she told me that she'd trained to be an actress I offered to pay for acting lessons in New York. I wanted to encourage her, to help her and Alistair put their bad luck in England behind them.'

'You must have been delighted, then, when she landed a part in the play *Love Betrayed*?'

'I was very pleased for her and I even went and saw it on the first night. She's a very fine actress, and as you may have heard, the play's now gone to Broadway.'

'Do you know the names of the producers of that play, Mr Morrow?'

'On Broadway?'

'No, off-Broadway, when it first started.'

'No, I don't think I do.'

'Perhaps you would kindly look at this programme then, and refresh your memory.'

The programme was handed over to the witness box and Morrow read through it.

'Have you ever heard of Come Tomorrow Productions?'

Alistair was sure that the American hesitated for the first time in giving his evidence. 'No, I can't say I have.'

'Are you sure?'

'Sure I'm sure.'

'Because I put it to you that Come Tomorrow is a pun on your name and that you put the money up for this play.'

'That's not true.'

'I invite you to consider your answer, Mr Morrow, because in precisely two hours' time the New York police will be interviewing the director of the play about the source of its finances and I have no doubt that properly encouraged he will be forthcoming. Well?'

'Okay, I did finance it. Alistair had no money and, well, you know how it is, Claudia was desperate to get into acting, so I decided to help out. It was meant to be a fatherly gesture and the only condition was that Alistair was not to be told.'

'And Madame Rye went along with this?'

'Of course. Nobody was hurt by it and look what a success she's been.'

'It was your idea to use Ramirez as your stable jockey?'

'Yes. He had ridden for me with great success in

America and when I decided to expand my racing interests in Europe I asked him to go and live in France and ride on a retained basis.'

'And you paid him an annual retainer fee for that purpose?'

'I did, at the beginning of each season, and in addition he had the right to a share in any of my horses which were sold as stallions.'

'And is that all the payment you gave him?'

'That's all. Of course he had his winning percentages which were not inconsiderable.'

'What about the packet you gave Mr Rye every month to deliver to him which you said contained an additional cash payment in dollars?'

'I know nothing about such payments.'

'You don't remember them? Large brown packages weighing a couple of kilos or more?'

'I have no idea what your client is talking about.'

'It was your idea that Sunday after the Deauville race to get rid of Ramirez?'

'Yes. I was unhappy with the way he had ridden Philanderer and told Alistair he was to tell him that his retainer would not be renewed the following season.'

'And then you left for Paris by private plane, arriving at your hotel there, the Plaza, at 5.15, or thereabouts?'

'That's right.'

'Did you go out for dinner that night, or eat in?'

'Neither, as a matter of fact. I had an early flight to New York the next day, and since I had enjoyed a big meal before the races I decided to give supper a miss.'

'And did you take any calls in your room that evening?'

'No, I turned in early and gave the switchboard instructions I was not to be disturbed.'

'So is it right that the only call you made was that in the early evening to La Cage to talk to Alistair?'

'That's right. Sometime about 7.00, 7.30.'

'I have your statement to the police here. In that you put it at about 7.15.'

'I wouldn't argue with that.'

'You made that phone call from your room, according to your statement.'

'That's right.'

'And first you spoke to Claudia, and then to my client?'

'Absolutely right. And I have to say neither mentioned a fight or anything like that.'

'Why are you lying about the phone call, Mr Morrow?'

The American reacted angrily. 'What do you

mean by that? I'm telling this court the truth. You can check my hotel bill.'

'I intend to, because, thanks to the Commissioner of Police, I have a duplicate here from the hotel. It says you made one call costing 30 francs.'

'And that would be the call to La Cage.'

'Are you sure? Because I also have here the computer print-out for telephone calls from your room that night.' The lawyer produced a sheet from the table in front of him. 'A very useful device for monitoring the number and length of every phone call made from the hotel.'

Morrow had now regained his composure and answered confidently: 'Then it will no doubt show that I made a call to La Cage lasting several minutes.'

'It does indeed. But there is one detail which you unfortunately overlooked, because it also shows the precise time the call was made. A wonderful thing, science. That call was made at 5.20 p.m., before my client even saw Ramirez. So where were you, I wonder, when you made the call at 7.15 p.m.?'

Morrow did not reply.

Pression was in no mood to wait for an answer. 'Could you tell the court why you needed to hire a car during your short stay in Paris?'

'I didn't.'

'Could you then explain the Mercedes that Hertz arranged to be waiting for you at the rear of the hotel that evening, in which you somehow managed to drive three hundred kilometres? I have the documentation here in my hand, if you wish to check it.'

Again Morrow chose not to answer.

'Your silence says it all, Mr Morrow. I suggest that it was you who had been using my client, in his innocence, to carry drugs into France believing he was carrying cash payments for your accomplice Ramirez. And that when the English jockey was caught, you decided that Ramirez was likely to become a danger to your safety; that you and Claudia Rye had become lovers and that when you phoned her that night at 7.15 she told you what had happened and you used it as a means to frame my client; to put into effect an escape route which you had planned many months previously by opening an account in his name in England and arranging funds to be transferred there from a fictitious account in Switzerland. Finally I put it to you that when you made that second call you were no more in Paris than my client, but a few kilometres down the road, waiting to murder your jockey when he returned to his home. What is your answer?'

'Just prove it.'

* * *

After Alistair had given his evidence and withstood a rigorous but by now less enthusiastic cross-examination by the prosecutor, the judges and jury retired to consider their verdict. After all, it was still Alistair who was on trial. Two hours later they returned and with great solemnity the poker-faced president of the court delivered their decision. Not guilty sounds good in any language.

Chapter 23

By the following weekend Alistair was happily ensconced in Amy's London flat, whilst Morrow and Claudia were having to suffer the less salubrious surroundings of a French police cell. Alistair's dramatic acquittal did not of itself mean that his employer and wife would automatically take his place in the dock. The examining magistrate, dashed of the expected satisfactory end to his investigation, had merely authorised their arrests, pending further police inquiries. These were to include forensic examination of the boot of the car which Morrow had rented and used to transport Ramirez's body, and an investigation into the American's financial affairs in America.

Maître Pression had now wormed his way into the confidence of Inspector Renard – or possibly it was the other way round, once the inspector had discovered that the commissioner of the Paris police was related to the lawyer – and had been told that Claudia was singing like Edith Piaf in her Deauville cell. Apparently her affair with Morrow had started shortly after she and Alistair had moved to New York and it had been the American's idea to set Alistair up as the fall guy should his heroin-smuggling operation ever be discovered. Claudia had also offered to give evidence against her lover, but the police were understandably apprehensive at the prospect, even suspecting that Morrow was behind the suggestion. What jury would convict on the words of a proven liar?

Further details of Morrow's past had also begun to emerge. His second wife had died in mysterious circumstances from a drug overdose and there were remarkable similarities between the manner of her passing and that of Eddie James's. Both Alistair and Amy were now convinced that Morrow and possibly even Claudia were responsible for that jockey's demise. Alistair remembered how he had telephoned Morrow from Newmarket and told him of his proposed visit to James's flat. His employer, who had arrived with Claudia that morning from New York, would have had ample opportunity to pop over to Putney from their hotel before travelling on to Newmarket.

Alas, no one would ever know just how much the jockey really knew.

Alistair's most immediate problem was money. Under the circumstances he could now hardly expect Morrow to pay for Maître Pression's legal fees and his present bank account – excluding the mystery deposit account, of course – was well into the red. For the time being he was dependent on Amy's charity and whilst she seemed delighted to support him, it was not a state of affairs his pride would allow to continue for too long. What he really wanted was to start training again, but that required capital into six figures, and in the meantime he scarcely envisaged any rush to employ him as a racing manager. Before he could plan his future, however, there were a couple of matters from the past which he was determined to clear up – Hassan and Stride were scores which had to be settled.

The police inquiries into the shooting of Willie Grange appeared to be getting nowhere slowly. Amy's suggestion that they should look into Hassan's movements had also resulted in a dead end. The fat Moroccan had a perfect alibi for the whole afternoon – he was watching the races from a private box and had several witnesses to prove it. The only person who could finger him was the man who had pulled the trigger, and, in no doubt that it was Hassan's dirty work, an attempt to kill Riding High which had literally misfired, Alistair decided that there was no alternative but to pay a further visit to Tissot.

Unfortunately Willie himself was still in no fit state to join the outing, but the other lads were brimming with enthusiasm for the idea. They met up on a Sunday night outside the flat in Elephant and Castle.

Tissot's decision the following morning to turn Queen's Evidence against his employer took the Metropolitan Police by surprise, but not Alistair. It was remarkable, he reflected, looking at his own scarred finger, how the proximity of a pair of pliers can loosen someone's tongue.

As for Stride, revenge was going to prove a little more difficult. Alistair still had the contents of the package which Willie had removed from his office, and was steadfastly resisting Amy's suggestion that they should be consigned to the rubbish bin. He certainly had no intention of blackmailing his former owner, but he hoped that he could at least cause him a certain embarrassment if a suitable occasion arose. He readily accepted that such a sentiment was wholly unworthy, and that angered Amy all the more.

They were lying in bed one Sunday morning reading the papers when Amy let out a yell. 'Look.

Alistair, it's a photograph of Stride and some young man.'

Alistair leant over to look at what was the gossip page of the paper in question. 'Go on,' he said, 'read out what it says, then.'

'"Millionaire racehorse owner Max Stride is hoping to be elected to the Jockey Club within the next month. He is pictured here with his friend and business partner, Charles Tucker. Five years ago Stride inherited a fortune from his father, an East End property dealer, a fact he doesn't like to mention too often in front of his friends in fashionable circles."'

'Christ!' Alistair exclaimed. 'Stride to become a member of the Jockey Club and me lying here unemployed.'

'Cheer up!' said Amy. 'Why don't I write to him saying you're going to sue him over that horse you bought for him in Keeneland?'

'It's a complete waste of time. He'll never pay and all he'll do is make threats again.'

'At least we can have a try. Leave it to your lawyer.'

A week later they were out having dinner when Amy called for a bottle of champagne.

'What are we celebrating?' asked Alistair suspiciously.

'I've got a letter here for you from Stride. Go on, open it.'

Alistair opened the letter and to his astonishment pulled out a cheque made out to him for the sum of $1,000,000.

'Is this a joke? Stride would never have signed this. Amy . . .'

'Oh but he did, and with enthusiasm. You see, I sent him a full-blooded lawyer's letter asking him to honour his obligation to pay for that horse and suggested that he telephone me at work to discuss the problem as a matter of urgency. He called the following morning and started swearing at me down the phone and saying he had no intention of paying. I just listened and said fine and then asked him what he wanted you to do with that package which Willie had borrowed from his office. I said you were most anxious it shouldn't get into the hands of the senior steward of the Jockey Club. Funny, isn't it, how people's attitudes suddenly change?'

Alistair laughed. 'And the package?'

'That goes back to its rightful owner as soon as that cheque you're holding has been cleared.'

As he kissed her and then the cheque the future suddenly seemed very rosy.

More Thrilling Fiction from Headline:

JOHN FRANCOME

STUD POKER

'Francome writes an odds-on racing cert' *Daily Express*

When Paul Raven's ride at Plumpton crashes through the
wing of the third last flight, it seems like one of racing's
tragic but unavoidable accidents. But that doesn't explain
why Paul's closest friend, the charming ex-amateur Alex
Drew, appears to be involved. Or why the fall that ends
Paul's career should finally destroy Alex.

Paul discovers a link between what happened at Plumpton
and a sequence of other bizarre accidents apparently
connected with a private poker school run by the wealthy
but embittered property developer Clay Wentworth. Fellow
players include a sinister Czech businesswoman whose
laser firm is developing a profitable sideline; a rich, ageing
rock star and an unsavoury Mr Fixit, Digby Welcome.

Stud Poker, lasers and moneyed decadence seem to have
little to do with the world of National Hunt racing, but by
the time Paul is caught up in the dangerous game, other
less honest players have stepped forward. And the stakes
are high...high and deadly.

'Skilfully tailored and easy to read' *Sunday Express*

'Talented, accomplished: a winner!' *Oxford Times*

DON'T MISS John Francome's previous bestseller, STONE
COLD, and with James MacGregor, BLOOD STOCK and
DECLARED DEAD, also available from Headline

'Authentic and appropriately fast-paced' *Books*

'A thoroughly convincing and entertaining tale' *Daily Mail*

FICTION/CRIME   0 7472 3754 9